confessions of a
teen nanny

confessions of a
teen nanny

A Novel by Victoria Ashton

HarperCollins*Publishers*

A PARACHUTE PRESS BOOK

Library of Congress Cataloging-in-Publication Data

Ashton, Victoria.
Confessions of a teen nanny / by Victoria Ashton.— 1st ed.
p. cm.
Summary: Drawn into the glamour, luxury, and romance of Manhattan's elite by the sister of
one of their charges, two sixteen-year-old nannies enjoy high salaries, extravagant gifts, and
attention—for which they may have to pay a very high price.
ISBN 0-06-073173-7 — ISBN 0-06-077524-6 (lib. bdg.)
[1. Nannies—Fiction. 2. Wealth—Fiction. 3. New York (N.Y.)—Fiction.] I. Title.
PZ7.A8295Co 2005
[Fic]—dc22
2004018283

2 3 4 5 6 7 8 9 10
❖
First Edition

To Fanu, Ale, Sasha, Reg, and J Jo—
without you all, I never would have been
the most popular girl in school!

Contents

CHAPTER ONE

how on earth
did I get into this mess?

*D*ecember

Adrienne Lewis raised a Baccarat champagne glass and proposed a toast: "To a great party and the worst night of my life."

Across the empty room, Adrienne's best friend, Liz Braun, raised her glass and nodded. "You got that right."

"Tonight didn't turn out the way I planned at all," she said, half to herself and half to Liz. Adrienne looked around the incredible penthouse at 841 Fifth Avenue, the scene of an enormous party she and Liz had just thrown.

The apartment was famous in New York for its elegance, its size, and the fact that it was owned by the billionaire socialites Dale and Christine Warner and their daughters, Cameron and Emma. Adrienne and Liz both worked as nannies in the building. Adrienne had started with the Warners a couple of months ago, watching their eight-year-old daughter Emma. Liz worked for their neighbor, Dr. Mayra Markham-Collins, a prominent child psychologist and author, who had two children, Heather, age nine, and David, age five.

"More champagne?" Liz asked, waving the half-empty bottle at her friend. "We have tons left, and there's a load of food in the kitchen. Pâté? Caviar? Doritos?"

"No, I'm cool," Adrienne said, wishing the queasy feeling in her stomach would go away. Wishing she could rewind the night and figure out how the party had gone so horribly wrong.

Liz stood up and shook out her curly, dark hair. She smoothed her hands over the peach Chanel cocktail dress, conveniently "borrowed" from Mrs. Warner's amazing closet. Slipping her feet back into the Jimmy Choo heels that Adrienne had swiped for her from seventeen-year-old Cameron Warner's shoe closet (*more like a shoe store*, Liz thought), Liz walked over to her friend, and the two girls surveyed the wreck that was now the Warners' apartment.

Adrienne took a deep breath. "If we don't clean this apartment *immediately*, I am so *totally* fired."

Liz nodded. "Okay. Let's get to work. We can have this place back to normal in no time. It will be so clean, Mr. and Mrs. Warner will never know we had a party."

"That won't be too hard," Adrienne said. "Mr. Warner

is *always* drunk. He won't even notice he's *home!*" They ran to where their clothes were stashed in one of the apartment's guest rooms near the Warners' master bedroom suite.

Slipping out of the Dolce & Gabbana designer dress Cameron Warner had given her, Adrienne sighed, smoothed out the wrinkles, and put it back on a hanger.

I look so great in these clothes, she thought. *I can't believe Cameron has so many. It's not fair.* She tried to control the anger bubbling up inside of her. When it came to Cameron, *nothing* was ever fair.

She placed the dress in the wardrobe, where Cameron always hung the clothes she was sending out to have cleaned. The bills from Madame Paulette, the dry cleaner, frequently came to thousands of dollars a month. The Warners would never notice the extra cleaning.

Back in jeans, the girls finally looked like what they really were: high school students after a night of partying without permission. Turning up the music, Adrienne and Liz emptied the ashtrays, straightened the paintings, and cleaned the bathrooms.

"Adrienne?" Liz called from across the apartment. "Someone hurled in Mrs. Warner's toilet!"

"Well, flush it!" Adrienne called back. "And stop yelling. You'll wake up Emma!"

Adrienne kept thinking about her boyfriend, Brian, as

she cleaned. Kept thinking about what she had seen before he left.

"The bathrooms are spotless, and all the shoes and accessories are back in Mrs. Warner's room. Do you think we're almost done?" Liz came in and asked Adrienne.

"Pretty close," Adrienne replied, dragging two huge bags of garbage into the service elevator area. "Tania gets here about six in the morning." Tania was the Warners' Russian housekeeper, who watched Emma when Adrienne wasn't working. Adrienne glanced at the clock. Three A.M.! "Tania will give this whole place another once-over. Mr. and Mrs. Warner will go straight to bed. They won't even check the living room. And they'll never go in the kitchen—I don't even think Mrs. Warner has ever *seen* inside the kitchen." Adrienne looked around the enormous room with its incredible views of the city, TV area, and casual dining corner. The Warners' kitchen was bigger than her family's *apartment*. "By the time they wake up, it will be like this whole thing never happened."

"I only wish that it would be like it had never happened for both of us," Liz said. "You know, you should go check on Emma, and then just run through each of the rooms and make sure someone didn't go into Mr. Warner's den, or Mrs. Warner's dressing room or bathroom, or something like that."

"Good idea," Adrienne said. Liz was always so practical.

Adrienne walked down a long hall off the entrance to

where the girls' bedrooms were located. Cameron's was sleek and modern, filled with contemporary art and books that Adrienne doubted she had ever even opened. Cameron was one of the most beautiful young socialites in New York, but she was not known at her school, Pheasant-Berkeley, for her major intellectual contributions. Liz and Cameron went to school together, and Liz had told Adrienne *plenty* of stories about Cameron over the years.

Adrienne carefully opened the next door and looked in on Emma. Tiny, blond, and snoring slightly, the eight-year-old girl was squeezed into a ball at the top of the bed, her sheets and covers crumpled on the floor. Smiling, Adrienne gathered them up and carefully placed them on top of Emma, who rolled over with a sigh. Emma was really adorable. *It's too bad she's an evil genius,* thought Adrienne.

Adrienne backed out of the room carefully and closed the door as quietly as she could. The *last* thing she needed was for Emma to wake up and start asking questions. Emma was a born prosecutor.

Walking back into the hall, Adrienne picked up the note that Mrs. Warner had left for her on the hall table. The distinctive paper on which Christine Olivia Warner wrote all her notes was pale gray. The card inside the envelope was thick, and at the top, her carefully engraved initials C.O.W. were in ivory ink. The initials always made Adrienne smile.

Adrienne, began Mrs. Warner, *thanks so much for looking after Emma on such short notice.*

Short notice indeed, Adrienne thought. She had just been on her way out the door of her own apartment that morning when Tania called. Tania warned that if Adrienne wasn't at 841 Fifth Avenue in ten minutes, Madame Warner would fire her.

When Emma's asleep, first make certain that the curtains in the drawing room are closed. Mr. Warner hates coming home and finding them open.

Sure, Adrienne thought. *What she hates is the neighbors seeing him stumbling home drunk from some high society benefit.*

Adrienne walked into the drawing room. The room had high ceilings and was filled with gilt furniture that Mrs. Warner had told her had belonged to Marie Antoinette, the last queen of France.

Turn off the lights, shut down the bar, lower the Picasso over the flat-screen TV . . . Adrienne ran through her mental list as she walked around the room, finally pressing the hidden buttons that automatically closed the heavy satin curtains. As the curtains closed, she looked longingly out the window at the incredible views of Central Park and the glittering city. She pulled herself away and went back to the letter.

Finally, would you turn down our bed properly, and make sure that all the lights are out in my dressing room? Tania always forgets. You're a huge darling. Thanks. C.O.W.

Adrienne entered the bedroom, inhaling the fragrance of the linden-blossom–scented water from France that Mrs. Warner insisted be used to wash her sheets. Adrienne looked at the colorful walls, covered in a beautiful old wallpaper she had heard had been taken out of some English duke's country house. Adrienne lay down on the huge four-poster bed and felt the incredible silk cover and linen sheets. She closed her eyes. She wanted nothing more than to sink into a deep sleep and forget what had happened with Brian. *If I stay here, I'll fall asleep until morning,* she thought. Adrienne got up and quickly repaired the damage to the placement of the throw pillows. She pulled back the sheets and turned down the bed for Mr. and Mrs. Warner, smoothing the covers carefully.

You left a wrinkle! Adrienne could hear Mrs. Warner's brittle voice in her head. She was always yelling at the maids for not turning down the sheets properly.

Finally, Adrienne thought. *I can turn off the lights in the Cow's dressing room, go back to the kitchen, and watch TV with Liz.*

Adrienne opened the doors to Mrs. Warner's dressing room.

She ran her fingers over the incredible dresses and the dozens of fur coats as she entered the fantasy room. There were custom-built drawers, places to sit, and a whole room for shoes.

Unlike in any other closet Adrienne had ever seen, Mrs. Warner's clothes were stored as complete outfits in garment bags. All around the room, sealed garment bags hung on racks, all identical pale gray suede, with COW embroidered on them in ivory.

Next to Mrs. Warner's dressing table was a series of photo albums, which Adrienne knew contained photographs of the socialite in hundreds of outfits, fully accessorized from hairstyle down to the shoes. Above each picture was a number; the same number appeared on one of the garment bags, and in the bag was the complete outfit from the book. Every season, stylists from all the major designers came to the apartment with racks of clothes for her to choose from. The things she liked ended up in gray bags.

Like bodies at the morgue, Adrienne thought.

Next to the clothes books was a slender volume that Adrienne had looked at many times. Inside were pictures of Mrs. Warner's jewels—pages of diamonds, sapphires, rubies, and pearls, which were contained in color-coded leather drawers in the safe in the back corner. Adrienne looked over at it.

The safe was *open.*

Adrienne walked up to the safe carefully, her breath coming in quick, short gasps.

All the drawers were open. Many of the jewels were

shoved around in their trays, and some were even on the floor. In the middle, several pink leather drawers were open and empty.

Oh, my God, Adrienne thought. *Someone at the party stole Mrs. Warner's jewelry!*

With trembling hands, Adrienne opened the jewelry book to see what had been in the empty pink leather drawers.

Harry Winston Suite, read Mrs. Warner's loopy handwriting. *One necklace, one pair of earrings, one ring, and two bracelets totaling 250 carats of flawless, fancy pink diamonds. Tenth-anniversary gift from Dale.*

A scream rose from Adrienne's throat and echoed throughout the cavernous apartment. She slumped down on the floor of the closet in shock. *I can't breathe,* she thought, *I'm going to faint.* Her heart pounded in her chest in terror.

In seconds, Liz was there. She took in the situation quickly. Adrienne could only point at the safe. The *open* safe.

"Okay, stay really calm. Could Mrs. Warner have left the closet looking like this?"

"Never," Adrienne said, her green eyes welling up with tears. "She's so totally careful about her jewels."

"Adrienne, we have got to call building security," Liz said quietly. "We can't call the police, because the building hates that—they don't want any bad publicity. We'll get security up here right away, and they'll figure out exactly what happened." Liz hurried to the kitchen, where the building phone was located.

Adrienne nodded as her friend left her, not trusting herself to speak. *I may throw up in this closet,* she thought, *but I can't. Mrs. Warner will kill me.* The thought made her laugh out loud. *I can throw up all I want. Mrs. Warner is going to kill me anyway!*

Suddenly she heard a noise, and Adrienne turned.

"Oooo!" a voice said. "You are in so much trouble!"

Standing in the doorway to the dressing room was little Emma, dressed in tiny Lilly Pulitzer pj's, her hair in rumpled pigtails. Hands on her hips, Emma looked around her mother's closet. She closed her mouth, swallowed, and glared at Adrienne.

How on earth did I get into this mess? Adrienne asked herself.

CHAPTER TWO

u r a nanny!

*T*wo *Months Earlier*

"So, I'm in calc," began Liz, "and Cameron is sitting in the third row, wearing these amazing Prada sunglasses—*fast asleep.*" Adrienne grinned at what she knew would be choice gossip.

"No way," Adrienne replied, amazed as usual by the behavior of the rich girls who went to her best friend's snotty private high school on the Upper East Side.

The mid-October sun shone with the last gasp of summer warmth as the best friends walked together through Central Park toward the Sheep Meadow. Ever since they were little girls, Liz and Adrienne had loved the meadow. They had had birthday parties there, had played there, done homework there and, in fact, had each gotten their first kiss on the broad, grassy heart of Central Park.

Now, of course, they spent less time there. After eighth grade, each girl had started a different school—Liz had received a scholarship to the Pheasant-Berkeley School for Girls, and Adrienne had gotten into Van Rensselaer High, the best public school in the city. They had changed a lot, but their friendship had never faltered. Liz was the cool, practical friend, cautious and wise, and Adrienne, the impulsive and emotional one, always ready for a party or good gossip. Adrienne knew they made a great team.

That day neither of them noticed the gorgeous weather. They were completely caught up in the latest scandal concerning Cameron Warner, a classmate of Liz's whose escapades Adrienne followed like a TV soap opera.

"So our teacher, Mrs. Dunn—" Liz continued.

"Is she the one you always say is a total bitch?" Adrienne asked.

"Exactly. So Mrs. Dunn goes, 'Um, Cameron?' and wakes her up. Cameron gives Dunn the *total* look of death, *reaches* into her bag, and pulls out a bottle of Chanel polish and an emery board. It looks like she is going to start to do her nails!"

"Oh, my God!" Adrienne said, turning to Liz with a shocked expression. "No one could get away with that at Van Rensselaer!" She giggled.

"Well, no one gets away with it at P-B, normally," Liz said, and continued: "And so Dunn says, 'Cameron, if you spent less time doing your nails and more time on your calculus homework, you might actually pass this class.'"

"Outrageous," Adrienne said.

"But you'll never believe what happens next." Liz smiled and continued. "Cameron looks at her, takes off her sunglasses, and says: 'Mrs. Dunn, I am *not* doing my nails. This, for your information, is just routine maintenance. *I* don't do my *own* nails—somebody else does them for me. Furthermore, my housekeeper makes more money than you do.'"

"No way," Adrienne said, stunned. "Did she send her to the headmistress?"

"That is the scandal. No," Liz finished triumphantly. "Cameron *never* goes to the headmistress."

"I don't know how she gets away with that stuff!"

"I do," Liz replied. "Her trust fund. That and the new library her parents just built for our school."

Adrienne nodded. "I wish I were rich," she said. *Not that I'm poor,* Adrienne thought, thinking of the comfortable Upper West Side apartment where she lived with her family. "I wish I had extra cash for new clothes and going out with friends whenever I wanted—especially going out with Brian."

Brian Grady was Adrienne's boyfriend of two years. He was gorgeous, funny, smart, and broke. He lived in Washington Heights in a small apartment with his parents and three brothers. He always had to scrape together money when they went out.

"If I only had a job like yours," Adrienne moaned.

Liz worked three days a week as a nanny for Dr. Mayra Markham-Collins. Dr. M-C—as Liz liked to call her—had two kids, Heather and David, whose father's identity was still unknown. New York society whispered behind closed doors that they were test-tube babies. It was well-known that Dr. Markham-Collins wanted everything in her life to be perfect—including her children. Dr. M-C was rich, and Liz made a bundle. Adrienne envied her for it.

"Well," Liz said cautiously, "I was going to mention that to you."

"Mention what? How much money you make?" Adrienne teased.

"No!" Liz said, poking her friend in the arm. "There's another family at 841 Fifth, and they're looking for a temporary nanny for their daughter, Emma. She's eight, and totally smart—not a smart-ass like the kids I take care of. They just need someone two or three days a week for two weeks, until the real nanny arrives from London."

"Really?" Adrienne asked. "Work in the same building as you, with a kid who's not an alien? Excellent! How's the pay?"

"Better than what I'm making, that's for sure," Liz said. "The family is loaded."

Adrienne ran through the next two weeks in her mind. She didn't have any big tests—or any that she knew of yet. She smiled. "Liz, I'll do it. I can't wait."

"There's one catch . . ." Liz said carefully, glancing at Adrienne sideways.

"What's that?" Adrienne asked.

"The little girl, Emma?" Liz continued. "She's Cameron's half sister. The job is with the Warners."

"You're not serious!" Adrienne said.

"I am completely serious. They go through nannies like water. I swear to God, they have had, like, six in the past year since I started working for Dr. M-C."

"Why do they all leave?" Adrienne asked.

"Mrs. Warner is really demanding. Also, Cameron runs the staff ragged doing chores for her. If you become Emma's nanny, you just might also become Cameron's personal assistant," Liz warned. "But, again, the money is killer. Five hundred dollars a week."

Adrienne stared, her mouth open. *One thousand dollars for two weeks? Sign me up!* "I'll do it," she said.

"Great!" Liz said. "I'm psyched! Maybe we can watch the kids together?"

"Definitely," Adrienne said, hugging her friend. Then she stepped back. "Wait. Do you think they'll hire me?"

Liz looked her up and down. Adrienne was very pretty, with short, layered gingery hair and green eyes. She was tall and fine-boned. Since going to Van Rensselaer, her wardrobe had changed dramatically from when they were

15

kids. She had abandoned the tidy, preppy look of her childhood for the edgier styles admired at her competitive public school. Her low-slung cargo pants and hippie-style tops looked playful and great on her, but Liz knew they wouldn't pass muster on Fifth Avenue.

"Listen, Adrienne, don't take this the wrong way, but you can't go in there looking quite so street," Liz said. "You need to be more Upper East Side."

Adrienne took in her friend's appearance. Liz had always been pretty, with her curly dark hair, but since starting at P-B, she had really grown into her looks. She had a beautiful face, with very pale skin and dark, almost black, eyes fringed with heavy dark lashes. Liz had an innate fashion sense and wore the P-B uniform with little extra touches that made her stand out from the other girls. She wore the crisp, white uniform shirt buttoned up to the neck, where she tied a colorful silk scarf. The school's baby blue uniform sweater was made of some horrible yarn, but Liz had saved to buy a cashmere sweater that fit the requirements, which felt and looked better. One of the reasons Liz had taken the nanny job with Dr. Markham-Collins was so she could afford the kinds of accessories and clothes it seemed *all* of the girls at P-B had to have: Hermès scarves, pearl earrings, and expensive watches. The uniform skirt, an unflattering blue-and-white-plaid kilt, was an unavoidable evil for all the girls at school, but Liz rolled hers up to a sexier height that showed off her long legs.

Adrienne sighed. She loved her own look and didn't really want to be an Upper East Side clone. *It's only for two weeks,* she reminded herself. "What should I wear?" she asked.

"Wear that simple white blouse of yours, and those really slender gray pants you wore to my birthday party. That green sweater you have is great for your eyes, too. Get some cute flats, and you can borrow this scarf. You'll look great, and she'll think you go to school with Cameron." Liz smiled encouragingly. "Mrs. Warner would freak out if she thought a girl from a public school was taking care of her genius child."

"Hello!" Adrienne said, offended. "I go to one of the top-five public schools in the *country!* The graduating class at Van Rensselaer has more Ivy League acceptances than any school in the city, *including* yours."

"I know, I know," Liz said, "but how many of those kids have parents in the Social Register, houses in the Hamptons, or multimillion-dollar trust funds?"

Adrienne was silent.

"I thought so," Liz said. "Borrow my scarf." She handed the scarf to Adrienne.

Adrienne took it. The major cash was worth a stuffy scarf. "'Beware of all enterprises that require new clothes,'"

Adrienne said, quoting Henry David Thoreau, who was on her reading list that year.

"You'll be fine. You're so smart. The Warners will love you."

"You're the best," Adrienne said. "Hey, what time do you have to be at work?"

Liz glanced at her watch. "Oh, no! Ten minutes from now. I have to run. I'll call you as soon as I talk to the Warners' housekeeper."

"Text me on my phone," Adrienne yelled as her friend turned and ran across the great lawn of Central Park toward Fifth Avenue.

It had been hours. Adrienne was dying to hear what had happened with the job at the Warners'. Why hadn't Liz called yet?

She closed her World History textbook. There was no way she could concentrate on the Great Depression. She looked around her room, which was painted a funky green that she and Liz had chosen together. Schoolbooks and papers cluttered her desk, and her Matrix screen saver rippled in the fading afternoon light. She gazed out her bedroom window at the partial view of the Hudson River. She inspected the movie-poster–covered walls—anything to kill time. Suddenly her cell phone rang. Adrienne looked at the screen.

U R A nanny ! ! !

Adrienne screamed and dialed Liz.

"Hello?" Liz answered, sounding out of breath.

"I'm so psyched!" Adrienne cried.

"I'm grossed so out," Liz replied. "David keeps throwing up."

"Is he sick?"

"Only because he went into my bag and ate ten Mallomars. He'll be fine." She giggled. Dr. Markham-Collins's kids weren't allowed to have junk food, but Liz always brought some to bribe them so they wouldn't misbehave. "Trust me, when you're a nanny, you'll have moments like this."

"So, I have an interview?" Adrienne asked.

"Totally. You can go at three o'clock Friday afternoon after school. You get out at two forty-five, so you have plenty of time to get there."

"That's tomorrow!"

"You bet. Remember, dress up." Adrienne heard screaming in the background. "I have to go. Heather is freaking out. Oh, another thing: If Cameron is there, don't let her know that we're friends. She doesn't really like me very much, and it won't help you."

"No problem," Adrienne said. "Who knows? Maybe Cameron and I will hit it off!"

"I doubt that," Liz said, laughing.

"Don't laugh. I can handle a spoiled Upper East Side princess," Adrienne said.

"Just watch yourself," Liz replied. "See you after your interview on Friday. And Adrienne? Good luck!"

CHAPTER THREE

is this kid for real?

Adrienne walked up to the entrance of 841 Fifth Avenue and glanced at her reflection in the carefully polished glass. *Not too much makeup*, she thought. *I look good. Like a very young Nicole Kidman. Sort of.*

As Adrienne approached the door, it was suddenly pulled open by a uniformed doorman. He was extremely tall and wore a long gray wool coat covered with gold braid. *He looks like a ship's captain*, Adrienne thought, but smiled and offered him her hand. "Hello," she said, in what she hoped was a professional-sounding voice. "I'm Adrienne Lewis. I'm here to see the Warners."

The doorman looked at her with pity. Adrienne lowered her hand. *Well*, she thought, *so much for being nice to the doorman.*

"Are you a friend of Miss Cameron's?" he asked, staring down his nose at her.

Adrienne swallowed. *What should I say?* "Um, I'm a

friend of Miss Emma's?"

The doorman nodded, then picked up the phone. "I have a Miss Lewis here to see Miss Emma." He waited a minute, and then hung up.

"You may go inside. The elevator to the Warner residence is on your left."

Adrienne stepped into the cool, marble-clad gloom of the lobby and opened her mouth in astonishment. The ceiling was gilded and painted, and the walls were covered with huge marble slabs and heavy mirrors. A fountain in the middle of the lobby tinkled softly, and the orchids planted around its base were reflected in the rippling water. Large French doors led to a grassy interior courtyard she hadn't even known existed.

This was so *not* what apartment lobbies she was used to looked like. Her own building had shabby tiled floors and an elevator that screeched every time it opened. *An orchid would probably die of embarrassment to be seen in my lobby,* she thought, staring at the gorgeous room.

"To your left, Miss Lewis," said the doorman, pointing.

"Sorry," Adrienne replied, scurrying to the elevator, the door of which opened automatically when she approached it. She got into the elevator and, as the door closed, realized that she didn't know what floor the Warners lived on. She looked for the control panel and discovered that there wasn't one. The elevator began to move on its own.

The elevator must be programmed to go straight to their floor—now that's *security!* Adrienne glanced around. *Pretty,* she thought. There were several small paintings of flowers, and a tiny little bench to sit on. A small chandelier hung overhead. The elevator suddenly stopped, and the doors opened slowly. Adrienne looked out the elevator's open door.

This is unreal, she thought as she stepped out of the elevator car and into the Warners' apartment.

The entry hall was enormous, and they were obviously in the penthouse because the entire ceiling of the entry hall was a glass skylight through which the sun streamed onto mosaic floors. The room was mirrored, and a large crystal chandelier hung from the skylight, the sun bursting into thousands of rainbow-colored sparkles on the walls.

YIP! YIP! YIP!

Adrienne looked down. A small, strange-looking dog stood shivering and barking on the mosaic floor. It had long hair hanging from its ears and its tail, but virtually no hair on its body. *Does that dog have a disease?* she wondered. It bared its crooked teeth at her.

"BEE-SQUEE!" called a deep, loud voice. "Stop it!"

The dog growled at Adrienne one last time and ran off.

The man who had called out approached her. He wore a tuxedo.

"Is there something wrong with that dog?" Adrienne asked with concern. "It has no hair."

The man stared at her with disdain. "It is a Chinese crested terrier. They are very rare. His name is Bisquit. It means 'cookie' in French."

"I see," Adrienne said politely, realizing too late that that had probably not been the best way to begin the interview. She extended her hand again. "You must be Mr. Warner. I'm—"

"I am not Mr. Warner," the man interrupted. "I am Kane. Mr. and Mrs. Warner's butler."

"Kane what?" Adrienne asked.

"Kane is my last name," he said irritably.

"Oh, sorry . . . Mr. Kane," she said.

"Just Kane, no Mister. Butlers are always called by their last name," he replied, as if he were speaking to a child. "I suppose you are Miss Lewis."

"Yes. Sorry. You can call me Adrienne."

"Certainly, Miss Lewis. I'm sorry they sent you up in this elevator. In the future, you are only to ride in the service elevator, unless you are with Miss Emma or another member of the family. Staff does not ride in the same elevator with the residents of 841 Fifth Avenue. Follow me." With that, Kane walked out of the hall. Adrienne raced to keep up with his long stride. They passed through a room hung with huge paintings, a large library, and a dining room. Then, they came to a large door that opened into the kitchen.

"This is really the kitchen?" Adrienne asked Kane. The kitchen was beautiful. One whole side was a restaurant-sized cooking section with polished-steel cabinets and marble countertops. There were stoves with eight burners apiece, and several ovens. Obviously, the Warners had *big* dinner parties. There were windows on two sides, with views over Manhattan to the East River. On the opposite side of the room, in a corner, was a breakfast table, and in the center of it sat a beautiful bouquet of flowers in a cut-crystal vase. Nearby, several sofas and chairs were positioned around a huge flat-screen TV.

"Mrs. Oblonskaya, this is Miss Lewis," Kane said, gesturing to a woman in the kitchen.

"Hello! Hello!" The cheerful little woman burst out from behind the counter and wiped her hands on a towel. She was shorter than Adrienne and about four times wider. Her gray hair was held in a tight bun, and she wore a carefully pressed black maid's outfit with a starched white collar.

"My name Tatiana Oblonskaya. You will call me please Tania." They shook hands solemnly, and then she grinned, revealing that she had a sweet smile and one gold tooth. Adrienne smiled back and liked her immediately. Kane was a bit of an acquired taste.

"That dog is something," Adrienne said, as Bisquit ran in circles, alternating between yipping at her and running behind Tania's legs to hide. "Does he bark like that all the time?"

"Only at all the peoples. From the Devil he comes that Bisquit. I happy turn him to mush in oven. He bite. You careful. Miss Cameron love it only because he nasty like she be. She is. Sorry, she not so bad. Only doggie. So! You here by us. Good. I teach, you follow." Tania threw the towel onto the counter and led her back out into the dining room.

She picked up a heavy envelope and handed it to Adrienne. "Is note. You read," she said, and stood, waiting.

Adrienne opened the note:

Darling!

We are thrilled, thrilled, thrilled to have you! So pleased you are with us. Be an absolute lamb, help Emma with French, make sure she practices piano, make sure she gets clean, clean, clean, and send her to bed. You're an absolute treasure.

Christine Olivia Warner

Adrienne blinked. "Isn't there an interview?" she asked. "Don't I need to meet Mrs. Warner or Emma?"

"In plenty time you meet," Tania said. "Miss Emma, she yell at you now. I mean talk to you now. You meet. Come."

This is so not normal, Adrienne thought. *My mom would be all over someone who was watching her kid.*

26

Tania walked back through the library and the entry hall, pointing to door after door: "Is Miss Cameron's room. She never home. Is guest room. Is guest room. Is other guest room. Here is room of Miss Emma. You go in. I wait here for you." She gestured to the door.

Adrienne knocked lightly.

"Come in," said a child's voice. Adrienne walked in. Emma Warner sat at her desk by a large window that looked out over Central Park. She was tiny. Smaller than an average eight-year-old, with a little blond bob that was a bit severe for a girl her age. Fine-featured, she turned to look at Adrienne with the calculating eye of an adult. Uncomfortable meeting her gaze, Adrienne looked around the room.

The bedroom had pretty flowered wallpaper and a romantic canopy bed swathed in lace and chintz. The white-painted bookcases were covered with dolls. The room was a little girl's paradise. However, Emma's desk was piled high with books. Mounted on a stand over her head was a TV, on which CNN was playing. Adrienne took a deep breath, and introduced herself. "Emma? Hi there, my name is Adrienne. It looks like I am your new nanny."

"It may look that way," Emma said, "but you are far from hired. You can sit over there." Emma pointed to a small upholstered chair. Adrienne, not sure how to handle the situation, walked over to the chair and sat down. It was a mistake. The chair was a lot lower than it looked. It was child-sized, and Adrienne wasn't. Suddenly, Emma stood towering over her, holding a small pad and a pencil.

This is ridiculous, Adrienne thought, and began to laugh. She tried to get out of her chair, but realized that she couldn't without moving Emma out of the way.

"Um, Emma, I'm kind of stuck," Adrienne said, trying to rise. "Can you just move, a tiny bit, so I—"

"Have you been a nanny before?" Emma interrupted.

Is this kid for real? Adrienne thought. "No, but I have baby-sitt—"

"Fine. Where do you go to school?" Emma shot back like a prosecuting attorney on TV.

"I'm at Van Rennselaer, but—"

"A public school." Emma sighed. "At least it's a good one. How were you referred to us?"

This kid is too much, Adrienne thought. *I have to get up. I'm losing control of this situation.* "Liz Braun—" she began.

"Oh, Heather's nanny. She's a freak. Not your friend, Liz. Heather. She's insane. Clinically. I won't play with her, so don't get your hopes up that you get to hang out with your friend all the time."

Emma closed the pad, but didn't move. "You'll do. For now. I watch CNN while I work. I'm translating *Madame Bovary* from the French. Have you read it? Probably not. Now, at four o'clock . . ."

I can't let her walk all over me like this, Adrienne realized.

I need to get back in charge. She stood up, and in doing so, forced Emma backward.

"At four o'clock," she said, her voice firm, "you do nothing. For your information I have read *Madame Bovary* in English and in French. I would also appreciate it if you would lay off your criticism of Heather. She is not clinically insane, or she would be in an institution. I am here to take care of you, not here to be patronized by you, or to be spoken to in a condescending way."

I have a feeling that I'm not going to get this job after all, Adrienne thought. *This girl is going to hate me.*

Adrienne continued moving toward Emma, and kept talking to her slowly and carefully.

"I will go over your translation when you are finished, and then, your mother has instructed me to see that you practice piano. If you have done all of that by four o'clock, then what, exactly, is it you want to do?" Adrienne smiled at Emma the same way her own mother smiled at her when she was beaten during an argument.

Emma swallowed and stepped back. She was obviously not used to this. "Well, I don't need you to help me with the French, just to check it when I'm done. Also, I only practice piano for fifteen minutes."

"You're going to practice until you play your piece perfectly. What on earth is so important?"

Emma squirmed in discomfort. "*Oprah.*"

Adrienne smiled. "*Oprah?*"

"Tania and I watch *Oprah* every day."

"I love *Oprah,*" Adrienne said.

Emma smiled shyly, and Adrienne smiled back.

"You look almost finished with that," Adrienne said, glancing at the translation. "I'll go to the kitchen with Tania. When you're done, come and get me and I'll go over it with you."

"Okay," Emma said, the moment between them broken. "See you."

Adrienne backed out of the room, her heart pounding. *I won,* she thought. *I won.* Adrienne was thrilled. *I totally won that argument!* Then she realized: Who gets excited over winning an argument with an eight-year-old?

I must chill, she thought.

Tania waited in the hall. She smiled when she saw Adrienne. "You come to kitchen. I give snack."

They walked back to the kitchen together. Tania gave Adrienne the rundown on the previous nannies.

"Magda, she first. Miss Emma, she put her coat in microwave. Big stink. Louise come next. No one know what happen. She just leave screaming. Diane is three, but she steal from Miss Cameron, is fired. Still, but I think Miss Emma does it sneaky-like. Last one, Gladys. She Bisquit bite her leg. Was accident." Tania looked at Adrienne. "You be careful."

This is not a great beginning, Adrienne thought.

The two stepped into the kitchen together, and Tania poured her an iced tea and gave her a small piece of poached salmon inside a puff-pastry shell. It was delicious, and light as air. Adrienne didn't even like fish.

"Is Russian. *Coulibiac.* I cook good, no?"

Adrienne just nodded, when Emma came in. "Check it," she demanded.

"Check it what, Emma?"

Emma stared blankly, and folded her arms.

"Emma, look." Adrienne stood up and stared down the bossy little girl. "You can be a pain, and I can be mean—or we can work together. What do you say?"

"Check it . . . *please,*" Emma said, handing over the work. Tania raised her eyebrows, and Adrienne smiled.

She ran her eyes over the translation. It was unbelievably difficult. *Wow,* she thought. *She did a really good job.* There were no mistakes she could see—only one verb that was in the wrong tense.

"You have this verb in the passé composé. It shouldn't be," Adrienne pointed out.

"I'm glad you caught that. I put it in deliberately."

Adrienne looked at her. *This little girl is a piece of work,* she thought. *Testing me?*

"Piano, Emma. Now," Adrienne said.

Emma rolled her eyes and went into the living room with Adrienne behind her.

Adrienne swallowed as she looked around the room. The ceilings were high, and the tall windows overlooked Central Park. They were hung with long, cream-colored satin curtains, through which the afternoon light shone. The furniture was gilded, and obviously expensive. It looked like the kind of stuff in palaces in old movies—and there was a lot of it. *I'll bet you could have fifty people in this room,* Adrienne thought, *and they'd all have a place to sit.* By the window sat a huge black piano that gleamed. Adrienne couldn't imagine that Emma's hands were big enough to play it.

With a sigh, Emma sat down at the piano.

If I have to listen to scales every day . . . , Adrienne thought. She shook her head and reminded herself, *It's only for two weeks.* Suddenly, Emma began to play.

Adrienne's mouth opened. Emma was a genius.

Her fingers ran up and down the keyboard with surprising speed and agility. Adrienne had taken piano lessons for years, yet she had never gotten anywhere near as good. *I can't believe this girl is only eight!* she thought. *I think I'm going to quit the piano.*

Emma leaned into the keys, coaxing the beautiful Mozart piece from the instrument. Finishing with a flourish, Emma turned to Adrienne with a slightly anxious expression. "Can I watch *Oprah* now?" she asked. "*Please?*"

"*Oprah* it is," Adrienne said.

Emma beamed, and leaped from the piano seat. She raced back to the kitchen, and Adrienne followed her. Tania was waiting for them and had plates with cookies and glasses of milk ready. The theme music for *Oprah* came on, and Emma turned to Adrienne, grinning.

"Adrienne!" she cried. "Incredible weight-loss makeovers! Have a cookie and sit down—these are the best. Tania always cries."

"Big people get skinny and beautiful. Break my heart, I so happy for them," Tania said, nodding.

Adrienne joined them on the sofa. Bisquit came in and seemed surprised to see her still there. He jumped onto the sofa between Adrienne and Emma, who ignored him.

Adrienne gave Bisquit a piece of her cookie, and he looked at her adoringly through moist eyes.

Well, well, Adrienne thought. *It looks like I'm going to get along just fine.* She glanced around at the incredible room. *I can't believe how much money they must have,* she thought. *Liz never mentioned that this was like a palace!* Adrienne settled back into the soft suede-covered sofa. *I think I could get used to it here!*

CHAPTER FOUR

perfect in Prada

After *Oprah*, Emma was served dinner. She ate early because her mother liked her in bed early. After dinner, she began to get nervous. "It's almost seven," she said. "My mother will be coming soon. You'd better get me into my bath. She'll freak out if I'm not in there."

"What time will she get home?" Adrienne asked.

Emma gave her a blank look. "She *is* home. She's in her room."

Adrienne blinked. "She's been in her room this whole time?"

"Of course," Emma said. "She needs her rest."

What is up with these people? Adrienne thought. *No interview, and leaving me here alone with her servants and her child? This is really weird.* Adrienne tried not to look too surprised. "Thanks for the clue," she said. "Do you need me to help you in there, or can I just run the bath for you?"

"Just run it. I use lavender soap. Not too hot," Emma instructed.

"You got it," she said, turning to go to Emma's bathroom.

"Oh, Adrienne?" Emma said.

"Yes?" she replied.

"That green sweater? My mother *hates* green. You need to change your sweater."

"Are you serious?" Adrienne asked.

"Very serious. My mom has fired people over less."

I can't piss off Mrs. Warner right away, Adrienne thought. *But who goes berserk over a color?*

"Hurry! You can borrow something from my half-sister," Emma said.

"Okay," Adrienne said reluctantly. "But will she mind if I borrow her clothes?"

"Mind?" Emma said. "She'll never even know."

Adrienne followed Emma down the hall, where they could just hear Tania and Mrs. Warner murmuring in the entryway.

The two girls slipped into Cameron's room.

Adrienne looked around. Like Emma's room, Cameron's had a huge window overlooking Central Park and the skyline. Unlike Emma's, the room was for no little girl. Stark and modern, Cameron's room looked like what Adrienne imagined a movie star's bedroom would be. On every wall, there were black-and-white fashion photographs of supermodels, most of them signed to Cameron.

"You'd better hurry before my mom finds us," Emma said, opening the door to Cameron's closet.

Adrienne's jaw dropped. It was like walking into an entire boutique at Barneys. Her eyes ran over the dozens of cashmere sweaters, which lined one bank of shelves.

"Quickly," Emma said again. "Take that pale gray one. It will look good on you, and Cameron will never miss it. She's so dumb, she won't even notice it's gone. Hurry!"

Worried a bit about taking the sweater, but even more nervous about making the wrong impression on Mrs. Warner, Adrienne grabbed the sweater and followed Emma back down the hall to her room. Emma went to take her bath and left Adrienne alone.

Adrienne took off the green sweater and put it on Emma's bed. She unfolded the gray sweater and noticed the incredible softness of the fabric. She held it up to her body and looked into Emma's dressing mirror. The mirror was short for her so she had to stoop a little. *It looks good,* she thought. Then, Adrienne noticed the label: Prada.

Oh, wow, Adrienne thought. *Prada. I'll bet this sweater costs over a thousand dollars.* She sighed. There was no time to risk going back to Cameron's closet. She pulled the sweater over her head.

The sweater fit perfectly, and the pale color brought

out her green eyes and red hair. Taking a deep breath, she decided it was time to meet Mrs. Warner.

As she stepped out of Emma's room, Adrienne got her first look at her new boss.

Mrs. Warner was very pretty—or had been once. Her skin was beautiful but very tight. *Maybe a face-lift?* Adrienne thought. Her blond hair was carefully styled, and her nails were manicured perfectly in a pale, natural color. She wore a pink Chanel tweed suit with black bows on it and stood on impossibly high pink and black shoes that showed off her gorgeous long legs. Finally, around her neck were the largest black and white pearls that Adrienne had ever seen. She couldn't even believe that they were real.

"Here she is," Tania said. "Miss Emma like her, and me, too."

"Adriana, how very nice to meet you," Mrs. Warner said, extending her hand. "We are so glad to have you on board. We've had such trouble with nannies." She smiled prettily. "I'm sure Tania has told you everything."

"Not really," Adrienne replied. Mrs. Warner seemed nice. "But my name is Adrienne."

"Oh, of course, dear. I'm so sorry. I've lost my head. Well, we *are* expecting a nanny in two weeks from London. We have the hardest time with the help here, and we can't have just anyone; as you can tell, Emma is a very special child. She needs someone very qualified. So when I asked

Dr. Markham-Collins if she knew anyone, and she recommended you, well, that was good enough for me."

Adrienne smiled. *What on earth did Liz say about me?* she wondered.

"Now, tell me about yourself," Mrs. Warner said.

"Well, I'm in high school. I've done lots of babysitting before—in my building or for friends of my parents. My parents are both professors at Columbia University. I'm an only child—"

"Great," Mrs. Warner said. "Let me just tell you *everything* about our little family. You won't really need to know all this, but I just want you to feel informed. No surprises." Mrs. Warner smiled. "Why don't you come into my office? We can chat there."

Adrienne followed Mrs. Warner through the apartment. She barely had time to look around. Mrs. Warner spoke so quickly, and seemed to want to tell her everything about their family before they even made it to her office.

"Mr. Warner works late and leaves early. You probably will never even see him, but you might see his son, Graydon. Gray is at Columbia, but he's always stopping by to eat the food or use the computer." She looked at Adrienne carefully. "He's not *my* son. He's from the first Mrs. Warner. The first Mrs. Warner was someone my husband met in college. After Mr. Warner made his money, she divorced him and kept the house, their friends, and the bank accounts. He had nothing! I tell you."

"I see," Adrienne said.

"Well, it took him years, and I mean *years,* to make the money back, and then who does he meet?"

"You?" Adrienne asked.

"No, dear, sadly for him. He met the second Mrs. Warner. She is Cameron's mother. A supermodel. From *nowhere.* I mean, she was practically a . . . never mind. Anyway, Cameron is her daughter. *Very* beautiful. I have high hopes for her. Well, *that* marriage ended, and now I am the third and *final* Mrs. Warner. We had Emma eight years ago. It's a real love match for us. I have, of course, been trying to make up for lost time. Mr. Warner never cared about the family's social position, so I have to do *all* the work. The right apartment. The right schools. The right friends. The right charities. And the right *nanny*," she finished, showing Adrienne into her office, which looked like a room at the Metropolitan Museum of Art. It was full of expensive furniture and paintings and many bouquets of flowers. She gestured to a small chair across the desk from her, sat down opposite from Adrienne, and continued talking.

"The children are very busy. Graydon is in his junior year and wants to go to business school. Cameron can't get this modeling bug out of her system. I'd really prefer her to be a debutante and marry someone nice. College is really for *other* people, don't you think?" she asked, not waiting for an answer. "I, myself," she continued, "generally wake up early, have Pilates training, and then a massage in the gym next to my bedroom. Afterward, my personal assistant, hairdresser, makeup artist, and stylist arrive around eight o'clock. I have a little espresso and go over my plans for the day."

Adrienne blinked. *That doesn't sound so rough,* she thought.

"Then, after some morning phone calls with my charities, I generally have a lunch date, and then I come home." Mrs. Warner smiled. "And that is when I really need you, Adriana."

"Adrienne," she insisted.

"Of course you are," Mrs. Warner said, getting up and moving to the door. "I need absolute peace and quiet while I rest. I never want to be disturbed. Sometimes I have important meetings in my office and I can't have interruptions of any kind. So I need a nanny to keep Emma occupied, and sometimes to stay with her in the evening if Mr. Warner and I go out and Tania isn't available. Is that all right with you?"

Adrienne nodded. *Doesn't sound too bad,* she thought.

"But why has it been so hard for you to find someone?" she asked.

Mrs. Warner seemed annoyed at the question. "Well, Emma is a prodigy. We're planning for her to begin high school by ten, and to graduate from Harvard at fourteen, so that she can devote herself to studying the piano. I need someone here every day for her. Every day."

Every day? Adrienne thought. *I thought it was just for two or three days.* She thought carefully. *I can hang on for two weeks.*

Mrs. Warner continued. "Well, that's all you need to know, and here you are for today." She handed her an envelope. "We'll see you on Monday, then?"

Yes! Adrienne thought with relief. *I got the job, and she didn't bust me for the sweater!* "Monday it is," Adrienne replied. "Thank you, Mrs. Warner."

"Oh no, thank *you*," she replied. "By the way, that's a gorgeous sweater on you. Is it Prada?"

"Yes," Adrienne said, but her mind whirled. *Should I admit that I borrowed it?* she thought, terrified that Mrs. Warner would recognize it as Cameron's.

"You young girls can get away with those severe cuts. Not me—I need something less hip," she said, turning to model her exquisitely tailored suit that showed her long legs to perfection.

"Oh, I think you could wear anything you wanted to, Mrs. Warner."

"You're a lamb. Thank you." Mrs. Warner led Adrienne out of the office and into the front hall, where they heard the clicking of high heels on the mosaic floor. Mrs. Warner turned to see who it was. "Oh, Cameron!" she exclaimed.

"I didn't know if you'd be in time to meet the new nanny, Adriana."

Adrienne turned in horror. *Oh no,* she thought. *Now I'm really busted.* Adrienne faced Cameron, prepared for the worst.

Cameron Warner was seventeen years old, but she looked far older than that. Five feet ten inches tall, she wore high-heeled Manolo Blahnik boots that pushed her over six feet. She was long and lean, with the scarily thin body required of fashion models. She had long, straight blond hair and perfectly white skin. Cameron posed in the archway with her purple Bergdorf and black Barneys shopping bags. Apparently, for Cameron, the world was her runway.

Cameron gazed right at Adrienne as she sauntered across the hall. *She is unbelievably gorgeous,* Adrienne admitted to herself. It was Cameron's eyes that were the most unusual. They were a pale silvery gray with a hint of aqua, and they held Adrienne's gaze intently. *Could they be contacts?* Adrienne wondered. Cameron wore jeans that fit perfectly and a white cashmere turtleneck. But she wore the simple outfit as if it were the most expensive outfit from Paris. *Who knows,* Adrienne thought. *If this sweater is any indication of what her clothes cost, those may be the most expensive jeans ever.*

"Some more shopping, darling?" Mrs. Warner asked.

"You know that your father asked you to tone it down a bit. Five thousand a month is really enough for school clothes."

Five thousand a month? thought Adrienne. *They wear uniforms at their school!*

"Whatever, Christine," Cameron said, walking right by Adrienne, dropping her bags on the floor, and scooping up the shaking Bisquit, who had run in. She walked over to her stepmother and they kissed each other, staying well away from each other's makeup. Cameron turned to Adrienne. "Who's this?" she asked.

"This is Emma's new nanny," Mrs. Warner said.

"It is *so* nice to meet you," Cameron said. "You look so familiar to me! Do you go to Pheasant-Berkeley?"

"No, but my friend Liz Braun does," Adrienne jumped in before remembering Liz's warning.

"Oh, Liz. Right," Cameron said without interest or recognition. "I guess I don't know you, then." She turned to go, and then turned back with a gleam in her eye.

"I guess it's just that sweater. I have one very much like it. But since mine was made especially for me by Miuccia Prada, it can't be. Mine is exactly the same color as my eyes. They custom-dyed the cashmere for me. I wore it to last year's Prada show in Milan." Cameron smiled.

I'm toast, Adrienne thought, and then the realization swept over her: *Emma set me up! She knew that Cameron would notice, but she told me she wouldn't!* Adrienne waited

43

for Cameron to expose her.

"Well, I'll let you two girls get to know each another," Mrs. Warner said. "I'm off to meet my husband at the Neue Galerie uptown. You'll make sure Emma gets into bed, won't you, Adriana? She's got to be in bed by eight or she's so crabby when Tania wakes her in the morning. Bye, girls." Mrs. Warner grabbed her purse off the table in the hall and walked into the elevator, which Kane held open for her.

Cameron turned to Adrienne. "Okay, what's your real name?"

"What?" asked Adrienne.

"Your real name. My stepmother is hopeless with names. She's famous in New York for forgetting them. The only reason she remembers mine is because it is the name of the town where my father made all his money— Cameron, Texas."

"How'd he do that?" Adrienne asked.

"Oil," Cameron said without interest. "Your name?"

"Oh, I'm sorry, I'm Adrienne Lewis." They looked at each other. "I'm so sorry about the sweater. It is yours." Adrienne started to offer an explanation.

"Don't worry. Let me guess. You were in green, right?"

Adrienne nodded. "I never would have borrowed it, but Emma . . . "

"Ugh, my little sister is a toad. She lives to get people

44

in trouble. Don't worry about it. You can keep it—I've been photographed in it so many times, I can't wear it anymore. Besides, it looks good on you." Cameron tilted her head to the side. "You know, you have amazing green eyes. If you reddened your hair a little more, you could really bring them out. I'll give you the name of my colorist."

"Well, thanks," Adrienne said, not sure whether to be offended or flattered.

"No problem. So, nice to meet you. See you soon. You'd better get Emma out of that bath. She always stays in until she gets pruny," Cameron said with a giggle and a wrinkle of her perfect nose. "Ciao!" She walked toward her room, sashaying on the heels of her boots like a runway model.

Emma had gone to bed without a struggle. She was exhausted.

Adrienne said goodbye to Tania, and Kane showed her into the service elevator. Once inside, she opened up the envelope Mrs. Warner had given her. Three bills fell out: three one-hundred dollar bills! Three hundred dollars. Per day! Sixty dollars an hour. One dollar a minute! Amazing! For a second, Adrienne wondered if Mrs. Warner had made a mistake. Then she thought about the apartment full of art, Cameron's five-thousand-dollar clothing allowance, and the plasma-screen TV in the kitchen, and realized that the money was for real and for *her*. She decided to splurge on a taxi.

The ride to Morningside Heights on the Upper West Side was quick, and as soon as she was home, Adrienne called Liz.

"It was awesome!" Adrienne said. "I got three hundred dollars for five hours' work, and Cameron gave me a Prada cashmere sweater made especially for her. It is *so* gorgeous, I can't stand it."

"Really?" Liz said, perplexed. "That doesn't sound like the Cameron I know."

Adrienne told her the story of Mrs. Warner's green-o-phobia and Emma and Cameron.

"Oh, I get it now," Liz said.

"What?" Adrienne said.

"It's just that Cameron probably gave you the sweater not because she was being generous, but because she would never wear it again."

"She said that," Adrienne admitted. "She said she'd been photographed in it a lot."

"Enjoy the sweater, Adrienne, but I wouldn't wear it to the Warners' again. Don't ever remind Cameron you owe her one. And I think the reason she won't wear it again is because she saw *you* wearing it."

"Are you serious?" Adrienne said, her feelings hurt. "Oh well, it's a nice sweater. Talk to you tomorrow?"

"You bet," Liz said. "Good night."

"Good night."

Adrienne looked at the sweater, which sat on her chair. It was so luxurious, it managed to make her whole room look really shabby, and suddenly, thanks to Liz's comment, it made her feel a little shabby, too.

CHAPTER FIVE

anything for *Oprah*

"**Y**ou cannot be serious!" shrieked Tamara Tucker, Adrienne's best friend at Van Rensselaer High. "That little girl Emma watches *Oprah*?"

"Seriously," Adrienne replied. "It really looked like she would have a fit if she couldn't. Maybe she's just addicted to makeovers."

"Emma is too funny!" Tamara exclaimed. All their girlfriends at the lunch table laughed. Adrienne smiled at Tamara. Tamara was usually the center of attention at their regular corner table. Popularity came naturally to her. She had been blessed with a dancer's body, gorgeous coffee-colored skin, and dark eyes that attracted the admiring attention of half the guys in their class. Plus, she had an unbeatable cutting-edge style.

But this week, nothing that Tamara had to offer could change the fact that Adrienne was now the undisputed queen of their table. After only three days on the job, her stories of the crazy Warners were already in big demand.

"Do the imitation of the Russian maid again!" Tamara urged.

"No, tell me about the apartment again," coaxed Adrienne's friend Lily Singh.

Adrienne launched into her description for the umpteenth time.

"I love it when you tell the part about the elevator with no buttons," Lily said. "I only wish my building *had* an elevator."

"In my building, the only pictures on the elevator wall are *graffiti*," Tamara said, cracking everyone up.

Adrienne laughed and looked up. Brian was standing there, smiling and waiting for her to finish. Even though they had been dating for two years, the sight of his deep brown eyes, wavy brown hair, and broad-shouldered body still made her heart skip a beat. He was so cute!

"You done?" he asked, holding out his hand to her.

"Completely!" she said. "Bye-bye, girls. I haven't seen him all day." The other girls hooted at them, as they walked away.

"Hey," Brian said, and smiled. "What have you been up to?"

"Telling stories from work. Can you believe that the Warners have Picassos and all this silver, and Mrs. Warner's jewelry is off the hook—"

"I know, I know," Brain interrupted. "I got your hundreds of text messages and e-mails. Remember?"

Adrienne blushed. "Okay. Maybe I'm getting a little carried away. But it is cool. Right?"

Brian shrugged. "I don't really care about their stuff," he said.

Adrienne reached out and squeezed his hand. Brain was the least materialistic, most down-to-earth person she knew. He never cared about the trendy clothes, the expensive sneakers, and all the other stuff their friends used to compete with one another. That was one of the things that made him so attractive. So sexy. He was *real*.

"So, besides all the stuff, what's the family like?" Brian asked as the headed down the crowded hall.

"Mrs. Warner is such a ditz. She can't remember my name at all, but Cameron says she's like that with everybody," Adrienne said. She kept her fingers intertwined with his as they navigated a path to his locker. She loved the way their hands fit together so perfectly.

"Sounds weird to me. How long are you working for them again?"

"It's just a week and a half more," Adrienne said. "Not long."

"Are you going there after school today?" Brain asked as he swung open the metal door of his locker. Adrienne marveled every time at how neat and organized his locker was. Only one month into school and hers was stuffed full of random papers, forgotten sweatshirts, and junk.

"Yes," she said. "Liz and I have been meeting in the park at the bandshell after school. We walk over to 841 Fifth together from there."

"When are you done?"

"About eight, why?"

"Let's go out tonight," Brian said suddenly, his brown eyes sparkling. "I have a science lab after school, then we can get a slice of pizza after you finish."

"I can't," Adrienne said. "I have to go to study hall now to see if I can get all my homework finished, and everything I can't get done then, I'll have to do at home, late, after I get back from the Warners'."

"Come on . . . I'll wait for you outside the building. We'll grab a slice, and I'll take you right home." He gave her a big smile.

"You're crazy. It's a school night. I said that I can't—"

Brian grabbed her around the waist and gave her a kiss right there in the middle of the hallway.

"Well, maybe *one* slice," she said, kissing him back.

Adrienne and Emma sat together at the round table in the Warners' kitchen while Adrienne stared at Emma's homework. Emma went to a school for gifted children, but she also got work from tutors who came every day.

51

Adrienne sighed. It was basic calculus, but it was practically what Adrienne was doing herself in class at Van Rensselaer. She stared at the equations, her mind reeling. *Whatever happened to normal second-grade 2 x 2 = 4?*

"I'm going to need a minute," she said to Emma. "Why don't you go practice, so we can get it all out of the way in time for *Oprah*? There's no reason for you to sit here staring at me while I try to work it out."

"Good idea," Emma said. "I wish my parents would get TiVo. It would make my schedule a lot easier. I'll be back in fifteen minutes."

Emma retreated to the living room, and Adrienne whipped out her cell.

"Hey there!" Brian answered. "You quit already?"

"Almost," she said. "I'm about to jump out the window over Emma's calculus."

"An eight-year-old is doing calculus?" he asked incredulously.

"Don't ask," Adrienne said.

"The rich are twisted," he said. "Eight-year-olds should be in the park. Hey, you and I should be in the park. Let me just get a pencil. Read me the equation."

Emma returned after Adrienne had gotten off the phone, and the two girls went over the math. Emma seemed pleased that Adrienne was able to explain something that had confused her.

"I knew the textbook was badly written. It couldn't be me." She grinned. "What time is it?"

"Time for cookies and *Oprah!*" Tania said, from behind the kitchen counter.

The three sat down on the sofa, and Tania started pressing the buttons on the complicated remote control for the TV. *Better her than me,* Adrienne thought. *I'd probably launch a space shuttle by accident with all those buttons.*

Nothing happened. The TV stayed blank.

"What's up?" Adrienne asked as Emma reached for the remote.

"Oh no, oh no. Is me, I do it again," Tania said.

"What?" Adrienne asked, confused.

"The satellite. Did you hit the satellite button again? It takes an *hour* to reset! An *hour!* Didn't you learn last time?" Emma poked at the control, becoming increasingly upset.

"It's a new episode! I can't miss it!" Emma's eyes watered up. "Adrienne, fix it!"

Adrienne stared at Emma. *Now this,* she thought, *this is* normal. *This is the behavior of a spoiled eight-year-old.* She glanced at Tania, who looked frantic. Adrienne took a deep breath. "Don't worry. I'll call Liz, and we'll go downstairs and you can watch *Oprah* at the Markham-Collinses. Okay?"

Emma began to calm down. "Okay," she said. "But you can't tell."

"Tell who?" Adrienne asked.

"My mother," Emma said quietly.

"Miss Emma can no allowed to watch TV," Tania explained. "I let her. Just a little bit."

Adrienne nodded. "Okay." She turned to Emma. "First, apologize to Tania for acting that way," she said.

"Sorry," Emma said in a petulant tone.

Adrienne picked up the phone and dialed.

"Hello?" Liz said.

"Crisis," Adrienne said. "Satellite is out. *Oprah* must be viewed."

"Understood. Come on down. Take the service elevator."

Emma and Adrienne hurried out the back door of the kitchen.

"Take the stairs," Emma advised. "The service elevator is slow, and they're right underneath us."

They ran down the stairs, and as soon as they entered the Markham-Collinses' apartment, Emma turned to Liz. "Which TV can I use? Keep me away from Heather. We have issues."

Adrienne looked at Emma and then at her friend.

"Hurry," Emma insisted, tugging at Liz's skirt. "I'm going to miss the first segment, and it's Beyoncé today."

"Library," Liz responded. "Straight through the dining room. The TV is behind the painting on the wall. Hit the button to the left of the door. The control is on the table."

"Thank you," Emma said politely, before running off.

"That girl is a trip," Liz said. "At least mine act like kids."

At that moment, a grim-looking little girl in a plaid skirt and blue sweater wandered in. She looked miserable. Her hair was dark, and even though she was a little bit bigger than Emma, she appeared rather fragile. Her eyes seemed worried, a cloud of anxiety hanging over her like a rainstorm. Adrienne assumed she must be Heather.

"Who's here?" she asked Liz. "I don't know these people. My sense of security is very weak right now."

Liz smiled. "Heather," she said calmly, "this is my friend, Adrienne. She and I have been friends since we were the same age as you and Emma."

"Emma and I are *not* friends!" Heather shouted. She took a deep and dramatic breath to calm herself. "I'm going back to my room now," she announced.

"Nice to meet you, too," Adrienne said, staring at the little girl as she left.

"Don't let her psycho-babble fool you for a second," said Liz, turning away from the door. "She's a total operator, and I can guarantee you that she's up to something. Come on, let's check on David. He's in the dining room."

"Lizzie!" he called out when he saw her. "I don't want to eat this soy burger."

David was five years old and adorable, with a bowl

haircut and a sweet expression. He was sitting alone at the huge dining-room table, looking sadly at what appeared to be a beige hockey puck on his plate.

Liz approached him and put her arm around his shoulder. "I know, sweetie, but your mom says you have to eat a snack to keep up your energy."

"But why?" he asked, pouting.

"It's very good for you. It's all natural."

Adrienne winced. *It's beige,* she thought. *Ugh!*

"I don't want it," he whined.

"If you finish, I'll give you gummy bears," Liz said.

"A little, or the whole package?"

"The whole package. Do you want me to sit here with you, or should we leave you alone?"

"Alone," David said, grinning, "so I can throw it away!"

"Let me know when you're finished," Liz said. "We need to make sure that no snoopy mommies can look in the garbage and see an unfinished soy burger!" She gave him a big smile.

"Okay!" he said. The girls went into the kitchen.

Adrienne looked at Liz in astonishment. "You just promised to pitch that burger," she said. "Are you crazy?"

"No," Liz said. "I really like David. You know, I took him to his pediatrician a few months ago, and he said he was becoming anemic. The doctor asked what he ate every day, and when I told him, the doctor was really pissed. He told me that this kid needs red meat from time to time, and not a diet of only soy and kelp."

"Did you tell his mom?" Adrienne asked.

"Of course I did," Liz answered, "but she has these wacko theories of how to raise children. She insisted that he could get all the protein he needed from soy."

"So what do you do?" Adrienne asked.

"Well, I've been sneaking him out for a real burger several times a week after school."

"Did it work?" Adrienne asked.

"You bet! He grew an inch and gained two pounds," she said proudly.

"What did his mom say?"

"That soy is a miracle product and she was going to write a book about how kids should eat nothing but soy."

"She'll make every kid in America sick!" Adrienne said.

"Not my problem," Liz said. "Let me show you the apartment."

The two girls walked through the rooms. The layout was basically the same as the Warners', but the ceilings were lower and there was no skylight in the hall. Dr. Markham-Collins's apartment was as spare and as empty as the Warners' apartment was stuffed full of things. The walls were beige, the sofas were beige, the carpet was beige.

Even the food here is beige, Adrienne thought. *Everything matches.*

"I like it," Adrienne said, though she didn't. It wasn't nearly as nice as the Warners'. "It's very Zen."

"It's been feng shui-ed," Liz replied.

"What's that?" Adrienne asked.

"A Chinese specialist came and determined where the energy flowed through the house, and they moved walls and added mirrors and water so that all of the good energy would be channeled into specific places in the apartment."

"So where is the good energy at?" Adrienne asked.

Liz giggled. "It all goes into her office."

"No energy for the kids, then?" Adrienne asked.

"Dr. Markham-Collins doesn't give any of her own energy to her children. Why do you think she'd let the apartment give any of its energy to them?" The girls laughed at the craziness of it.

Suddenly, two of the mirrors in the room sprang open.

"Liz!" bellowed a woman with a deep voice.

"Oh, no!" Liz whispered. "She's coming out!"

"Coming out of where?" Adrienne asked in a panic. She looked around.

"Her office!" Liz said. "Grab Emma! Get into the kitchen! She *hates* guests!"

Adrienne ran into the library, where, mercifully,

Oprah was thanking Beyoncé, and Emma was turning off the set.

"We have to go!" Adrienne cried.

"Why?" Emma asked, not moving.

"Dr. Markham-Collins is coming out of her office. Liz says we should scram. We can scoot into the kitchen."

"Don't worry. You're with me," Emma said calmly.

Adrienne stared at the little girl. What was Emma talking about? She grabbed her hand and began to pull her toward the kitchen. Adrienne turned and stopped. There was no escape.

Blocking their way to the kitchen was Dr. Mayra Markham-Collins.

She was enormously tall, slightly overweight, and wore a colorful printed wrap dress and a black cashmere shawl over one shoulder, held in place by a glittering brooch. Her hair was wild, dark, and curly, and her face was framed by enormous black glasses.

"Elizabeth," the doctor said in her tremendous voice. "All I ask is that I am allowed to work in my office without interruption. All I ask is that you deal with the children for a few hours. All I ask is for a little quiet. But what do you do? You let Heather bang on my door. You let some strangers in to watch television in the next room. You leave my son alone in the dining room, where he could easily choke to death on his soy burger."

She took off her glasses and, noticing Adrienne, changed her tone.

"I'm very concerned, Elizabeth. Are you all right? It seems to me that you must be angry at me, and these careless acts are really a way of expressing your anger at me and at my children. If you'd like to talk about these issues, I'd be happy to send my card to your parents so that we can arrange an appointment to do it."

Liz looked up at Dr. Markham-Collins. "I'm very sorry. It's my fault. My friend Adrienne works in the building and she had a problem, so I tried to help."

"That is commendable on your part, Elizabeth," Dr. Markham-Collins said dryly. "But, as you know, unscheduled playdates for the children are out of the question. . . . And this interruption, on today of all days. I have just received a call from *New York* magazine!" Her voice trembled. "I have been named one of the city's 'Top Working Moms—Women Who Do It All'!"

Adrienne saw Liz look down at the floor. She knew her friend well enough to see that Liz was trying her hardest not to burst out laughing.

Adrienne stared in disbelief. What on earth did Dr. Markham-Collins do to win such an award? She stayed in her office all day while Liz or the housekeeper picked up the kids from school, fed them, and even took care of them on weekends!

Suddenly, Emma interrupted. "Hello, Dr. Markham-Collins. Congratulations on your article! I'm Emma Warner." She smiled brightly.

Dr. Markham-Collins stared down at Emma, noticing her for the first time. The doctor's face, formerly pinched and annoyed, suddenly beamed with cheery kindness, and she walked over to Emma. "Well, Emma. So nice to see you. How is your mother? She's building a wing at my hospital! I have been telling her for years that you should come down and play with Heather more."

"That's nice of you," Emma said, grinning. "But I'm always so busy. Adrienne, I'm sleepy. Can we go home now?"

"Sure," Adrienne said.

"Oh, you don't have to go!" Dr. Markham-Collins said. "Don't you think you can stay and play with Heather?"

"Oh, I'm *really* tired," Emma said.

"All right." Adrienne jumped into the conversation. "We'd better go, then."

"Thank you so much for your visit!" Dr. Markham-Collins said. "I very much look forward to seeing you both again soon. Liz, you were a genius to invite them. Ciao!" With that, Dr. Markham-Collins returned to her hidden mirrored office, and the apartment grew quiet.

"You'd better go," Liz said, trying not to laugh.

"Talk to you later!" Adrienne said as she left. She suddenly realized that, much to her great shock, after Dr. Markham-Collins's, the Warner home seemed *somewhat* normal.

CHAPTER SIX

who *are* these people?

Adrienne and Emma entered the kitchen and were treated to the sight of Mrs. Warner yelling at Tania.

"Now Tania, how could you! Where did they . . . ? Oh! *There* they are." Mrs. Warner turned to stare at Emma and Adrienne. Her beautiful face was lined with anger, and her heels clattered across the tiled floor of the kitchen as she approached them.

"Adriana. If you cannot be trusted to keep my child in the house, why on earth would I consider keeping you in my service?" she said with a sneer. "We only ask that you help us for a short time. It is your first week here, and you give me a heart attack! Where have you been?"

Adrienne panicked. She decided that the truth was the best way out of the situation.

"I'm sorry, Mrs. Warner. The television was out, and since Emma did her calculus perfectly and played her Tchaikovsky without mistakes, I promised her that she could watch a little . . . um . . . educational TV as a treat."

"Emma is not allowed to watch television," Mrs. Warner said sternly. "Didn't I tell you that?"

"Actually," Adrienne said, "you didn't tell me that, and I'll make sure she doesn't watch any more, but it was educational, and so it wasn't too bad." She took a deep breath. "I apologize."

"Yes, Mother," Emma piped up. "It was a special on the development of music through trans-urban locations, with an emphasis on potential cultural and economic development."

Mrs. Warner blinked. "Well, that sounds fine," she said hesitantly, almost scared of Emma. "Anyway, I was on my way out the door, and I saw that Tania was leaving, and you and Emma were nowhere to be found. Never let that happen again. I'm just glad that you're all okay. So, Adriana, here are your instructions for Emma's dinner. We'll be back around twelve, and Emma should be in bed by eight. You can stay in the kitchen, watch TV, help yourself to anything in the fridge. See you later."

"But . . ." Adrienne hesitated.

"But what?"

"But I have to be home by eight o'clock. I didn't know that I'd have to stay late tonight," Adrienne said, thinking of all of her unfinished homework and her date with Brian. *My mom is going to kill me. And Brian is going to be so upset!*

"Adrienne," Mrs. Warner said, suddenly turning sweet and remembering her name, for once. "We hired you to be on call. Like a doctor. Even when you're not with us, you're part of our family. We call on family members to help us when things get crazy around here. Right, Tania?"

Tania nodded, inching backward toward the kitchen service elevator—it was obvious that she wasn't going to let herself get sucked into staying.

"Listen," Mrs. Warner said, smiling sweetly. "Normally Tania or Kane is here, but tonight they're both off. I'm so crazed, I just didn't notice. It shouldn't happen again, and I'll add an extra hundred to your envelope to make up for the inconvenience. Good. See you later!" Mrs. Warner picked up her sable-trimmed cashmere shawl and her purse, and hurried toward the elevator in the front hall, blowing them all a kiss.

"Hokay. I go now," Tania said cheerfully. "Bye, Miss Emma, Miss Lewis. See you morning time!" She ran to the service elevator and was gone.

I can't believe I have to stay here, Adrienne thought. *I don't even know where they went.* Adrienne looked at Emma.

"'The development of music through trans-urban locations, with an emphasis on potential cultural and economic development'?" she said.

"I had to think of something," Emma said. "What's for dinner?"

"No clue," Adrienne said. "Let's check the fridge and see what's there. I guess it's just you and me, now."

"It always is," Emma said.

After arranging dinner for both of them and setting Emma up in her room with the *Sunday New York Times* crossword puzzle, Adrienne went into the kitchen and called her mother at home to tell her about the unexpected late night.

"I don't like the sound of this, Adrienne," her mom said. "It's very careless of her, and a big imposition on you. How will you get home? When will you get home?"

"I have enough money for a taxi," Adrienne said. "Come on, Mom. This building is as safe as a fort. I shouldn't be home too late. I'll call you when I'm leaving. The doorman will put me in a taxi."

"All right, Adrienne, but I'm not happy about this. Make sure you do your homework after Emma goes to sleep. See you later," her mother said, and hung up.

Now I have got to call Brian. She picked up her cell phone and dialed.

"Yo!" Brian said. "I'm finishing up at school. You almost done?"

Adrienne sighed. "Not really. Mr. and Mrs. Warner went out, and I have no idea when they'll be back. I've got to cancel."

"That bites! I was looking forward to the pizza," he said. "Hey!" he said suddenly. "Why don't I come over? Your kid goes to sleep soon, right? When she's out, call me and I'll come over and hang until around ten. Then I'll go home, and it'll be cool."

"That's a great idea!" Adrienne said. "It's at 841 Fifth Avenue. Just ask for the Warners' apartment. Bring some ice cream, too. I'll call Liz. We'll make it a party."

"You're on. See you soon!" He hung up.

Adrienne called Liz. "So, I'm shafted, but I have an idea."

"What's up?"

"Mrs. Warner stuck me with Emma at the last minute. I was supposed to have a date with Brian."

"What are you going to do?"

Adrienne told her the plan.

Liz arrived after she had put Heather and David to bed and after Dr. M-C had emerged from her office hideaway.

"Come on, let's set up the counter!" Adrienne said.

The girls ransacked the fridge, pulling out the chocolate sauces and preserves they would need for sundaes. Going into the butler's pantry, they pulled out expensive crystal glasses and dozens of pieces of Tiffany silver to eat with. Finally, they set the counter with votives and turned on the stereo to a cool station.

"We should do catering together," Liz said. "This looks great!"

The buzzer rang, Adrienne went downstairs to sign Brian in, and soon the three of them were sitting at the counter eating.

"This apartment is awesome!" Brian said, happily digging in.

Liz and Adrienne looked at each other and laughed.

"Brian," Adrienne giggled, "this isn't the apartment— this is the kitchen!"

"You're kidding me," he said, looking around again. "Who has a living room and a dining room in their kitchen?"

"Come with me," Adrienne said, grabbing his hand. Soon, she and Liz were giving him the tour of the apartment, showing him all the rooms, the art, and the amazing things.

"I can't believe this place," he said. "Oh, man—check it out! Look at this bar!" He walked over to it and flicked a switch. Slowly, hidden lights came on that lit up all the bottles from below. It was like a bar at a club, with hundreds of colorful bottles.

"What do you say I make us some Cosmos?"

"No way," Adrienne said, laughing.

"I'd love a Cosmo," Liz said, sitting on the barstool. "My day was brutal."

Adrienne hesitated. She drank, sure, but only at parties where other kids brought beer. She had even nipped a bit from her parents one night when Liz slept over, carefully topping off the bottle with water. She wondered if it was stealing to drink the Warners' liquor? There was so much of it. They'd never miss it. *Why not?* she thought. "Pour me one, too," she said, and sat on the stool next to Liz.

Amazingly, Brian knew what he was doing. He expertly mixed the liquor in a shaker, and poured out two icy Cosmos into the crystal martini glasses. "Cheers!" he said.

"Wow! I thought I knew everything about you. Who knew you were a bartender, too?" Adrienne said, smiling. She loved that Brian was always full of surprises. "Don't you want one?"

"Nah," he said. "Cosmos are for girls. I'll have a beer." He pulled one from a refrigerator hidden behind the counter.

Adrienne sipped the icy drink carefully. She knew there was alcohol in it—she'd seen Brian pour in a lot— yet she couldn't really taste it. The drink was deliciously sweet. She glanced at Liz, who was taking big gulps. Liz had obviously had Cosmos before—probably with her Pheasant-Berkeley friends.

The three drank their drinks while wandering around the apartment, laughing and checking things out. Soon, Adrienne realized she was getting drunk. *I feel great!* she thought. *Warm and fuzzy.* The apartment suddenly seemed hot to her.

"Well, I should probably go," Liz said. "You two should have a little time alone, and that Cosmo hit me like a subway car."

"When do you get to leave?" Brian asked Adrienne, smiling lazily and moving closer to her as the three of them entered the hall.

"As soon as the Warners get back," she said, hesitating, because after the Cosmo, the words didn't come as easily as they should have.

Suddenly, the elevator door opened and out spilled two guys Adrienne didn't recognize—and *Cameron.*

"Who the hell are you?" one of the guys asked.

Adrienne stared in horror. She had no idea who he was.

"Cam!" he cried. "What's up here? Who are these people?" He stepped into the hall and moved toward Adrienne. Brian stepped in front of her.

Liz looked at the other guy who had come out of the elevator. Without a doubt, he was the hottest guy she had ever seen. His dark brown hair fell into his soft blue eyes. He had broad shoulders and a chest she could just imagine lying her head against. *He's so gorgeous,* she thought.

Cameron exited the elevator in a slightly unsteady fashion. "Hey!" she said, a beautiful smile spreading across her face. "Excellent! The servants are partying!" She stumbled into the hall and stared at Liz. "I know you! You're a P–B girl! Woooooo!" she shrieked, and held up her arms, rock-style.

Adrienne and Liz looked at each other, instantly sober.

"No, seriously. I'm totally kidding, I didn't really *mean* the servant crack," Cameron said, throwing her arms around Brian. "Guys, this is Liz, who goes to school with me, and this is Adrienne, who has the misfortune of being my troll half sister's nanny."

Adrienne heaved a sign of relief. Cameron was obviously cool with finding them there.

Cameron looked unsteadily at Brian. "Who are you?" she asked. "Don't know you at all!" She looked at Adrienne. "Is he yours?" she asked.

"He is," Adrienne confirmed. "He came to hang out after Emma went to sleep." Liz gave her a glare of warning, which Adrienne ignored.

"The employer is away, so the nanny will play," Cameron teased, glancing meaningfully at Brian. "Hey, don't worry, it's cool, *Adriana!*" She burst out laughing at her own joke. Then she stumbled into the living room. Everyone followed.

"Cam, stop being a drunken pain and introduce me to these ladies," said the guy who came in first.

Cameron stood up straight and did an imitation of an Upper East Side hostess. "Well, Mr. Graydon Warner, of the Texas Warners, please meet Miss Adrienne Lewis, of the nanny Lewises, and her friend Miss Elizabeth Something, of the Pheasant-Berkeley Somethings."

"He's your brother?" Adrienne asked.

"Half brother," she responded, dropping her coat and bag on the floor by the bar. "Not good-looking enough to be my real brother. Oooh, were you guys drinking Cosmos? Can you make them? How clever of you. I'd love one!" she said, linking her arm through Brian's. "You obviously know where the bar is! Make us up a pitcher!" Cameron tottered off to the living room, dragging a bewildered Brian with her.

"So, I'm Graydon Warner," the guy said, coming closer to Adrienne. He had dark hair, chiseled features, and wore an expensive cashmere blazer over his shirt and jeans. He was good looking, but something about him seemed too slick, too spoiled. "I go to Columbia. Oh yeah, this is my friend, Parker Devlin. Parker and I went to Dudley Academy together. He's a senior there."

Liz gulped. Parker Devlin—of course. Parker was legendary. She had never met Parker before, but she had heard of him. Every private school girl in Manhattan knew about Parker. He dated all the coolest and wealthiest girls. His father was a media mogul, owning a few of the city's newspapers and magazines, and even a cable TV station. Figures that Parker was gorgeous, too.

"Hi. I'm Liz. I go to school with Cam," she said, daring to use Cameron Warner's nickname from school.

"Cool," Parker said. "What are you guys doing here?"

"We were just hanging out," she said. "Adrienne is a genius and tutors Cam's sister, Emma. We were just waiting for the Warners to return from their benefit so that we all could go home."

"That's cool," he said again, looking at her with interest as the others followed Cameron into the living room to the bar. "Do I know you?"

"I don't think so," she said, smiling at him and tilting her head as if she were trying to remember him from somewhere. A piece of her hair fell in her face. *Oh, that is smooth,* she thought. *Hair in the mouth. Nice.*

Parker reached forward and gently brushed her hair behind her ear. "You're too pretty for me to forget," he said smoothly, "so I know this is the first time I've met you." Liz caught her breath and quickly searched her brain for the appropriate flirty reply. At that moment, Cameron came over with a cocktail shaker in her hand.

Ugh! Liz thought. *I can't believe she's interrupting now!*

"Hey! Come into the living room! Adrienne's guy is a wizard with the bottle. He's mixing up everything! Liz, come on in! It's a party—I'm calling friends!"

Adrienne caught Liz's eye from across the room and smiled.

Why not?

It had happened so fast. An instant party. Cameron, Graydon, and Parker had pulled out their cell phones and, in about a half an hour, a group of ten kids had arrived.

"Hey, welcome!" Cameron called to a beautiful girl coming through the elevator. Liz knew who she was immediately: Mimi von Fallschirm. *Princess* Mimi von Fallschirm. It seemed as if all the coolest girls from P–B were there, girls she had barely spoken to last year. And Parker—gorgeous Parker. Liz decided, right then and there, to be a lot bolder this year. Starting now.

"Cameron," Liz said, approaching the two girls, "this party is so cool!"

"I'm glad your friend thought of it!" Cameron said, her eyes sparkling. "And her cute boyfriend over there is a maniac behind the bar—he can make anything. You must get a drink, Meems."

Mimi headed to the bar, and Cameron draped one arm over Liz's shoulder. "Liz," she said, using her name for the first time, "you have to promise me something."

"Sure," Liz said. "What?"

"You have to drink this Cosmo—you look tense." Cameron giggled and handed her the glass.

"Cheers!" Liz took a big sip.

"All right!" Cameron said. "Now, Liz, we go to school together, and I don't know a thing about you. Tell me everything, and then I'll tell you about my friends—

especially Parker. Am I right?"

Liz blushed and glanced across the room at Parker, who was talking to a guy she didn't know. He caught her eye and grinned. "You're right!" Liz said, taking another swig of her drink.

CHAPTER SEVEN

deep breath.
keep your cool.

Liz left the hour-long music history class feeling as if a train had run into her head. Drums, drums, and more drums . . . followed by math, spanish, and history. By lunchtime, all she wanted to do was take two Advil, drink a gallon of water, and crawl into a hole in Central Park. This was, without doubt, the last time she would ever party mid-week. It was a miracle that her mother hadn't smelled her bad breath at breakfast.

Stepping outside of the school building, Liz put on her sunglasses and inhaled deeply the crisp fall air. She started to walk down East Ninety-third Street to the Salad Patch, the restaurant where she and her friends Jane Tremont and Belinda Martin went for lunch every day.

Belinda and Jane were Liz's best friends at P-B. They were both smart, funny, and well-off, but nothing like

Cameron and Mimi von Fallschirm. Cameron's and Mimi's parents were multimillionaires many times over. Jane and Belinda's families were, well, just regular rich, not crazy rich.

Liz was looking forward to telling Jane and Belinda about the evening when, suddenly, she noticed a Maybach gliding alongside her in the street. Liz turned to look at it. At P-B, the girls learned (though not in class) which cars were worth looking at, and with a price tag of $300,000, a Maybach was worth a stare.

Suddenly, the window rolled down and a blond girl leaned forward.

It was Cameron.

Liz winced, prepared for a scene.

"Liz," Cameron called. "It's Cameron, Cameron Warner."

Liz turned. She knew exactly who Cameron was.

"Hey," she said uncertainly as the car stopped.

"Where are you going?" Cameron asked in a friendly voice.

"The Salad Patch," Liz answered. "I was going to grab lunch with Jane and Belinda."

"Ugh!" Cameron said, laughing and opening the car door. "Lunch at the Poison Patch? Come to lunch with us! We're just zipping over to Park Avenue for lunch at Mimi's."

Liz stared. *Was this really happening? Was Cameron inviting her to Princess Mimi von Fallschirm's house for lunch?*

"Are you coming?" Cameron asked. "Or do you really prefer those crappy salads?" She raised her perfectly tweezed eyebrows.

Liz stepped forward into the car, taking a seat next to Cameron. *Jane and Belinda will understand,* she thought.

"Mimi, this is Liz. She was at the party last night." Cameron explained.

Mimi von Fallschirm looked at Liz with an approximation of a smile on her face.

"I'm so glad you guys called last night. I was at the opera with my parents," Mimi said, extending her hand, which glittered with several tiny sapphire and diamond bands. "It was so boring, I thought I was going to die. Then I got Cam's text about the party, told my mom I was sick, and came right over. So much more fun than *Tannhäuser*." She smiled. Mimi had long, straight, ebony-colored hair and skin that was so white, it was almost unnerving. Her nose, which was a little crooked, wasn't quite pretty, but it gave her face character. The imperfection didn't matter when you were a princess.

"We're just doing a quick lunch at Mimi's. I'm glad you could join us. I wanted to dish about last night," Cameron said, smiling.

"Do you always do this?" Liz asked, looking around

the car, which was more amazing than anything she had ever seen. The seats were covered in beige suede, and the details were all paneled in walnut. There were several TV screens, a bar, and even bud vases filled with flowers. You couldn't hear the motor, see the driver, or even figure out where the light came from. It was like sitting in a box at the opera. That is, if Liz had ever sat in a box at the opera.

"We try to do it once a week," Mimi said. "My mother's staff is the best in town. We get in and out of lunch in under an hour. Plenty of time to get back to school—though why we'd bother to go to gym after lunch is beyond me. So we generally skip it." She leaned back in the seat. "This traffic sucks. Living on Park Avenue is such a pain with all these cars."

"Try living on Fifth," countered Cameron. "At least you don't get all the *parades*. Honestly, all those Irish and Greeks and whoever marching past your house beating *drums.*"

"I still have a hangover from last night," Liz said, holding her head. "Don't even mention drums, *please.*"

Cameron and Mimi burst out laughing.

"Oh, my God," Cameron said. "Meems, didn't I tell you she was great?" And with that bit of flattery, Liz began to relax.

Mimi von Fallschirm's apartment was incredible.

"See?" Cameron said. "It makes ours look like a dump."

"Stop it, Cam," Mimi said, pouting, "you're embarrassing me."

The three girls entered the apartment. A sweeping staircase ran up three flights beneath an open skylight. Huge windows looked up and down Park Avenue. The black-and-white marble floor was so highly polished, Liz was worried they'd be able to see up her skirt. The whole place smelled sweetly of oranges—there were blooming miniature orange trees in white tubs up and down the halls. Every few feet there was a full suit of armor.

Liz tried to look blasé. *Deep breath,* she told herself. *Keep your cool.*

"The dining room is this way," Mimi said, her heels clicking as she walked down the long hall ahead of them.

"Isn't it excellent?" Cameron whispered to Liz. "You know, you're really lucky I managed to get Mimi to invite you. No one from P-B besides me has ever been invited to Prince von Fallschirm's. They're very choosy." She winked.

They entered the dining room. The walls were covered with forest green brocade and portraits of men and women in elaborate costumes surrounded by golden frames.

"Who are all these people?" Liz asked, taking in the huge chandelier and the mahogany table, which was surrounded by twenty-four chairs.

"Ancestors," Mimi said dismissively. "We have even more in the house in Vienna."

Liz looked at the paintings. Every person in them had the same slightly crooked nose as Mimi.

"They have a *palace* in Vienna," Cameron whispered as the girls sat down at a small table, set for three, by a huge window.

A butler came out and placed three tiny cups of truffled bouillon on the table in front of them. Liz watched Mimi carefully.

Mimi picked up a silver spoon with a round shallow bowl, impossibly small, and then used it to spoon up tiny portions of the delicate broth. When they were finished, tiny feta cheese soufflés were served, each collapsing as the girls ate them with gilded fish forks. Soon, the butler came out with a bottle of wine.

"At lunch?" Liz asked.

Mimi looked at her quizzically. "In Europe, if you have a meal without a glass of wine, you are considered uncivilized."

"Well, in America, if you're a high school student who has a meal with a glass of wine, you're considered a lush," Liz joked, and then realized she had gone too far.

Fortunately, Mimi giggled. "Oh, Cameron, she is funny! Thank you for introducing us! Walter, *Sie können nun den Weifswein servieren,*" Mimi said to the butler, who nodded.

"Sehr wohl, Durchlaucht, wie sie wunschen," he replied.

"What did you say?" Liz asked.

Mimi smiled. "I said, Walter, you may pour the white wine."

Walter poured.

"What did he say to you?" Cameron asked.

"He said, 'Of course, Your Highness, as you will.' Now. Let's talk all about the evening last night. Enough about me."

Liz sipped her wine, and gradually her inhibitions loosened. *Mimi is funny,* she thought. *Not stuck-up at all.*

Cameron was telling a story from last night about being drunk and crawling under the furniture to look for a lost contact lens.

"Gosh, did you find the lens?" Liz asked.

"Of course not, darling," Mimi said. "She was so blind drunk, she forgot—she doesn't wear contact lenses!"

The girls shrieked with laughter, and when they settled down, Cameron finally focused her cool gaze on Liz.

"So . . . last night was a blast," Cameron said. "Parker's definitely hot for you."

Liz blushed, suddenly feeling like a Miss America contestant having a crown placed on her head. "Really?" Liz asked. "You think so?" She tried to sound cool, as if the hottest guys in New York were always after her.

"Completely. If he asked you out, would you go?"

"Of course," Liz said. "But what are the chances of that?"

"Don't sell yourself short, darling," Mimi said. "My mother was just an American. And *she* became a princess. Continue, Cam."

"All I'm saying is, if he asked you, would you go?"

"You bet I would," Liz replied too quickly.

"Then consider it done. I'll ask him to ask you out," Cameron said, leaning back into her gilded chair.

"You're not serious, are you?" Liz said.

"He thought you were hot. Parker's an old friend, you're a new friend. I see no reason not to."

"Cam, you're the best!" Liz said.

Cameron smiled and glanced at Mimi.

"Liz," she said, smiling slowly and pouring Liz another glass of wine, "you have to tell us all about your friend Adrienne. She's not one of us, but she's very cool. We really like her—don't we, Mimi?"

"Yes," Mimi said, leaning closer to Liz. "Such *energy.*"

"Have just a touch more wine," Cameron said to Liz. "How do you know her?"

Liz began telling her new friends all about Adrienne. About how the two of them had grown up together, and how they were still best friends.

"Is Brian her boyfriend?" Mimi asked.

"Yes," Liz said, sipping her wine. "They've been together for two years."

"Two years!" Cameron cried, tossing back her head

and laughing. "I can barely stand a guy for two weeks!"

The three girls laughed, and Cameron turned back to Liz. "Seriously," she said, putting her elbows on the table and her head in her hands. "You have to tell us how she does it. What is Brian really like?"

Cam and Mimi are so cool, Liz thought, and before she realized it, she was revealing the intimate details of her closest friend's private life.

CHAPTER EIGHT

today we turn you into a goddess

The campus of Columbia University swarmed with students. All over the lawns and paths, grad students and undergraduate students talked, ran to class, and studied under the trees and on the flights of steps to the academic building, which rose like a Greek temple at the center of the university.

"You've got your notebooks?" Adrienne asked Emma.

"Yes," Emma replied.

"You've got your pencils and calculator?"

"Yes, yes. You can go, Adrienne. I'm fine."

"All right. Have fun." Adrienne watched the little girl climb the steps to Lewisohn Hall for the Thursday afternoon "Gifted Teen Think Tank" of Columbia University, in which Emma was the only person who was not, in fact, a teen at all.

"Tania will pick you up at six," she called.

"I know," Emma said, irritated, and stomped up the rest of the steps without saying good-bye.

As soon as the door closed behind her, Adrienne was suddenly sad. She realized that today was actually the last day that she would see Emma. She had finished her two weeks. *And what a two weeks this has been!*

Hopping into a cab, Adrienne zipped from the bustling Morningside Heights location of Columbia University across the top of the park and over to Fifth Avenue. When Adrienne had started to work for the Warners in mid-October, it had still been warm. But now, only two weeks later, all the trees were turning brown. She looked up at the limestone curtain of apartment buildings and admired the Metropolitan Museum and the Frick Collection as she sped downtown. She had started to get used to this neighborhood and the crazy rich people who lived there.

I might actually miss them, Adrienne thought, pulling up to 841 Fifth Avenue and getting into the service elevator for the last time. All she had left to do was collect her money.

Entering the kitchen, Adrienne heard the familiar sound of Mrs. Warner having a meltdown at Tania in the front hall.

"Oh, Adriana, is that you? Thank God you're here! Please come in," Mrs. Warner called. Adrienne hurried into the front hall. "Could you be an angel and stay on for just another month? The nanny hasn't come from London as expected, and I am just in a bind, bind, bind! Something about her work visa." Mrs. Warner handed her an envelope. "This is what we owe you for the past week, and a little something to say thank you—also, forgive me, a little advance bribe, in the hope that you can stay on. Go ahead, look at it."

Adrienne peeked inside the envelope. There was a sea of hundreds. More than a thousand dollars!

"If Emma wants me to, I'm happy to stay on," Adrienne said, slipping the envelope into her jacket.

"Oh, thank God!" Mrs. Warner said. "You are an absolute TREASURE! I have to dash. Drinks at the Colony Club. Ciao!" Mrs. Warner left in a hurry, almost as if she expected Adrienne to change her mind.

"So you stay!" Tania said. "This nice. You come kitchen. I snack you."

Adrienne smiled and was just about to follow Tania back into the kitchen, when the elevator doors opened and Cameron fell into the front hall, covered in bags from Chanel, Gucci, and D&G.

"Oh . . . my . . . God!" Cameron said, giggling. "I think I have to go to the hospital. I think I broke my arm shopping!"

Adrienne helped untangle Cameron from the bags.

"Ugh. Heavy," Cameron said, smiling. "So, what are you up to?"

"Well," Adrienne admitted. "This was supposed to be my last day, but your mom said that the nanny who was supposed to come couldn't make it, and she asked me to stay on for a month longer." She grinned. "Well, I was just about to have a snack and go." Adrienne turned toward the kitchen. "See you."

"Where are you going?" Cameron asked.

"Home, to finally do some homework. I'm totally behind."

"Do you always work?" Cameron asked. "Don't you ever have fun?"

"I think you saw me have *too* much fun last week, Cameron," Adrienne said, laughing.

"No. You're not going home. You're coming with me."

"Where are you going?" Adrienne asked.

"Where are *we* going?" Cameron said pointedly. "*We* are going to heaven."

"Is that a club?" Adrienne asked.

"Sort of," Cameron said. "But *so* much better."

"Where is it?" Adrienne asked.

"Fifty-seventh and Fifth. Some people call it Bergdorf Goodman, but *I* call it heaven."

Stepping out of the limousine, Adrienne looked up at the facade of New York's most exclusive department store. She had been inside with Liz a few times, but they had always left empty-handed—she had once seen a moisturizer for a thousand dollars there!

"Come on in," Cameron purred, stepping out of the limousine. "The water's fine. You have enough time for a makeover, right? Every girl does. You need some glamour, Miss Nanny, and a serious kick-ass dose of it. Follow me. Today, Cameron Warner is your fairy godmother."

Cameron entered Bergdorf's like a ship in full sail, with Adrienne trailing behind her like a dinghy.

Adrienne's eyes widened. The salespeople literally tripped over themselves to get to Cameron.

"Miss Warner," said one, "perfume today?"

"No thanks, Carlos," she said, batting her eyes at him. "Today is a face-and-hair day. Ciao, sweetie."

They stood in front of the elevator, and Cameron flipped open her cell phone. "Hi," she cooed. "I'm here!"

Within seconds, two women met them at the elevator on the main floor. They were well-dressed and perfect-looking: perfect hair, perfect makeup, perfect designer clothes, perfect smiles. In fact, Adrienne thought they looked like robots.

"Adrienne, this is Petra, my personal shopper here at Bergdorf's. And this is Zoya," she said, gesturing to the other woman. "Zoya will be yours." Cameron blew a kiss to Adrienne as she turned to leave.

"Where are you going?" Adrienne asked. She felt as if

she were being abandoned in a foreign country where she couldn't speak the language.

"Don't worry, I'm not leaving you. The clothes won't be right on you until you get your total look. There is no point in shopping until your hair and makeup are done. Zoya will take you up to the John Barrett Salon, and she'll oversee the cut. Do whatever she tells you. She's the best."

I completely can't afford this, Adrienne thought, panicking. Then she remembered: She had more than a thousand dollars in cash in her pocket. The idea of all that money belonging to her made her a little giddy. She glanced back at the door. She knew she could make an excuse and leave. But Cam had brought her here. This is how Cam spent time with her friends. Adrienne didn't want to say no. She stepped into the elevator. And besides, there was no way a haircut could be *that* expensive.

"I am Juan!" the colorist announced. He spun her around. "Today, we turn you into a goddess. Your hair, it will be like flaming sunsets! Like the change of seasons!" He continued for so long that, by the time he was finished talking, Adrienne was really afraid.

My hair is going to look like a pile of dead leaves, she thought.

Then, Nils, the stylist, took over. Adrienne grew a little calmer.

After the cutting and blow-drying ceased, Adrienne noticed Cameron standing behind her. Cameron, if possible, looked even better than ever. "Cameron," Adrienne said, "you're so blond! You're amazing!" She admired Cameron's almost platinum-blond hair, softened by hints of pale gold.

"I know," she said without any pretense at modesty. "The Palm Beach season starts any minute. I had to put the sun-kissed streaks in there before the chlorine did it to me. Nothing on earth is worse than coming out with green hair in a picture in the *Palm Beach Post*'s color supplement."

"I can imagine," Adrienne said, even though she couldn't.

"Well," Nils said, putting the last bit of product in her hair. "You ready, Adrienne?"

"I guess so," she said.

Nils turned her chair around, and Adrienne looked at herself in the mirror.

She didn't recognize herself. Her unruly, flyaway hair fell around her face in sleek, silky chunks. Bangs drew attention to her eyes, which suddenly appeared blazingly green. The color of her hair had gone from a gingery brown to a real red, laced with streaks of honey and chestnut. It was amazing. *This,* Adrienne thought, *is me. This is how I am supposed to look.*

"Fabulous!" Cameron announced, pronouncing the final word on the transformation. "Adrienne, you're gorgeous.

Juan, Nils, Zoya—you are the best. Now, let's do some damage downstairs. Adrienne, prepare yourself. I am a trained shopping professional—do not try this alone."

The two girls went through the store like predators. Prada, Narciso Rodriguez, Chanel, Dolce & Gabbana.

"Adrienne, try these on." Cameron threw her three wrap dresses and a miniskirt in quick succession.

Adrienne glanced at the beautiful things. *There is nothing I would like better,* she thought, *but why bother?* There was no way she could afford them, and trying them on would only make her feel worse.

"Adrienne, please, you're bringing me down!" Cameron scolded. "Why the long face?"

Adrienne took a deep breath. "Well, Cameron, I'm really not sure these clothes are me. I mean, look at this miniskirt—it has less fabric than a washcloth."

"It's hot," Cameron agreed, nodding her head. "What you need is a pair of thigh-high boots to go with it."

"Cameron, did you hear me? I can't really use these things," Adrienne said.

Cameron looked at her. "Adrienne, I heard you, but I just don't care. You see"—Cameron leaned forward and whispered—"no one needs these things. They just *want* them. I hope you're not worried about the money—I don't pay for these clothes, and neither will you." She smiled.

Adrienne froze. "You're going to steal them?" she whispered, her heart pounding.

Cameron laughed hysterically, leaning on a mannequin in a beaded evening ensemble for support. "No, you idiot! They *give* them to me."

Adrienne blinked. "Really?"

"Seriously, Adrienne," Cameron said, quieting down and letting go of the mannequin, which had begun to rock perilously on its platform. "The reason I go out every night of the week is to make sure I get photographed by the press. I do that to keep my family's name in the papers. It doesn't reflect badly on my dad—a wild child gives him something to talk about at his stupid board meetings. My stepmom gets a little edgier about it. She's a social climber and *really* wants me to be Debutante of the Year." Cameron rolled her eyes.

"So your parents buy you the clothes?" Adrienne asked, still confused.

"Well, they do give me a monthly clothing allowance, but that is for the stuff I *need*: riding clothes, things for Palm Beach, ball gowns, stuff for dinner parties. You know."

I wish I did, Adrienne thought.

"But this stuff"—she gestured around the store—"these are my crazy clothes. These are the things that I wear to clubs, to restaurants with my friends, you know—things to hang out in." She grinned.

"So, who pays?" Adrienne asked.

"Bergdorf's. Barneys. Jeffrey. Wherever I shop. They know that this is the kind of stuff I get photographed in, and when the photographers ask me what I'm wearing, I tell them who designed it, and where I bought it, and then, the next day, in the paper, there's a picture of me and it says, 'Socialite Cameron Warner at Blah-blah Club, wearing Alexander McQueen, available at Bergdorf Goodman.'"

"That's amazing," Adrienne replied.

"So what I'm saying, Adrienne, is to take whatever you want. We're almost the same size. They'll never know it's not for me. Now, put on that miniskirt and show the world you have legs, please. Those cargo pants you always wear are atrocious."

As they continued shopping, Cameron talked about the pressure of growing up a Warner. "I guess I seem icy to some people. I can't help it. I'm actually pretty shy," she confessed.

Adrienne looked at her in astonishment. Cameron Warner? Shy?

"It's true," Cameron continued. "My therapist says I wear sunglasses so people can't see my eyes. I feel protected that way. The clothes give me more confidence than I have. My stepmother puts a lot of pressure on me."

"Well, I see she puts a ton on Emma," Adrienne confided.

"Emma can handle it. She's a supergenius."

"Pressure is pressure," Adrienne said, feeling bad for Cameron for the first time. *Poor Cameron,* she thought. *She's really kind of sad.*

"Anyway. Enough of that," Cameron said. "Oh, you know what? I had the nicest time with your friend Liz. She's really great. She came over to Mimi von Fallschirm's for lunch last week. You know what? I promised to set her up with Parker. He's an old friend, and I think he really likes her."

"Cameron, that's so great of you!"

"I know. I have no boyfriend of my own, but I'm happy to get them for other people. I'm an absolute saint!" she cried, striking a pose that was anything but saintly. "Hey, tell me about your boyfriend. What's his name?"

Adrienne smiled. "Brian. He's a brain, but he's so cute. He's really intense, he loves music—"

"We should all go to a concert sometime," Cameron interrupted. "I can get great tickets."

"We kissed for the first time at a concert," Adrienne admitted. "Radiohead. It was a little noisy, but so romantic."

Cameron smiled. "That's cute," she said. "Tell me more about him—"

"Excuse me, Miss Warner," Petra said. "It's almost nine. We'll be closing in a few minutes. Would you like me to pack up these bags?"

"Absolutely," Cameron said. "Listen, Petra. Load this pile into my car and give that other pile to Adrienne. She's taking them for . . . um . . . alterations." She winked at Adrienne.

"That's fine, Miss Warner." Petra hurried off with the clothes, and Zoya followed her.

Cameron gave Adrienne a little hug as she was leaving. "Thanks for coming," Cameron said. "When Mimi and I go shopping, she only wants to shop in Chanel. Can you imagine? Chanel is for old ladies. See you!" Cameron whirled, and left.

Adrienne stepped onto Fifty-seventh Street and began to walk west toward the subway. She wondered if she should just spring for a taxi. She still had hours of homework to tackle. The distinctive ring of her cell phone cut into her thoughts.

Adrienne struggled with her shopping bags to find her phone in her shoulder bag.

"Hi, it's me. Where have you been? I've left you messages." Brian sounded hurt.

"Bri, I'm so sorry! I was at the Warners', and I got stuck with Cameron."

"I figured that," he said. "Listen, I'm bored. I've been sitting at my desk all afternoon. I need to get out. You still owe me a late-night slice."

"I haven't even started to study—"

"You work too hard. Come on—a quick slice. Just you and me."

Adrienne hesitated. She knew she would probably have trouble concentrating on her math problems, anyway. *I'll wake up early and study*, she promised herself. "Sure," she said. "I'll see you at the pizza place on my corner in ten minutes. I'm just getting into the subway."

"Excellent," he said cheerfully. "See you then."

———————————

"Whoa!" Brian said when Adrienne entered the pizza place near her apartment. "What happened to your hair?"

"Do you like it?" Adrienne asked, dropping her bags onto the bench across from him and sliding into the booth.

"It's . . . sexy," he said. "You look hot." He leaned over and kissed her.

"Cameron got me a makeover," Adrienne said. "You won't believe how she's treated at Bergdorf's. It's like she's royalty or something. It's so cool."

"What's in all those bags?"

"Some things Cameron gave me," Adrienne said, reaching over and pulling a cute Marc Jacobs dress and a Theory top out of a bag and holding them up.

"They look expensive," he said.

"They are," Adrienne said with a smile. "And they look *great* on me."

Brian shook his head and frowned.

"What's wrong?" Adrienne asked.

"Nothing. I just think that you are too into their money, that's all. I mean, the Warners—Cameron—they're just people, like you and me. No big deal."

Adrienne laughed. "They are *not* just like you and me."

"See? You're blinded by all their stuff," Brian said. "Sure, they have a great apartment, lots of jewelry, whatever. But what do all those fancy clothes really get you?"

"Power . . . fame . . . popularity . . . come on, you can't tell me that Cameron doesn't look hot," Adrienne said.

"She's a type. I hate types. I like real," Brian said.

Adrienne rolled her eyes. "Oh, please . . . "

"Okay, maybe some guys would say she's hot," Brian conceded. "Not me."

"Why not?"

Brian leaned over and kissed her, hard. He kissed her again and again, his mouth melting into hers. He finally pulled away and said, "Because I want you."

CHAPTER NINE

arrive late, leave early. make an impression.

It's finally Friday. What a relief, Liz thought as she herded Heather and David into the elevator of 841 Fifth Avenue. Heather had been whining ever since Liz had picked them both up from the Karl Steinbach School.

"My foot hurts," Heather said, her lip trembling and her voice quivering. "I think I'm going to die of toenail cancer."

"Toenail cancer?" Liz said, trying hard not to laugh. Steinbach was a school that prided itself in developing the emotions of its students by exposing them to challenging experiences and information. Liz had always thought the kids at Steinbach were sensitive, but they were also the most neurotic kids in New York City. Heather was a born hypochondriac.

"Heather, there is no way you have toenail cancer.

There is no such thing as toenail cancer." She bent down to look Heather in the eye.

"There isn't?" Heather asked uncertainly.

"No. Is there anything bothering you that you want to tell me about?"

"Well . . . " Heather sniffed. "Bunny Crawford dropped a book on my foot, and it really hurt. She has displaced anxiety, and she used me as a surrogate for releasing her misplaced emotions of hostility against her mother."

"So you're telling me that your friend Bunny dropped a book on your foot?"

"Yes." Heather sniffed again.

"Then we have good news. You don't have toenail cancer. You have an actual hurt foot. I bet when we get upstairs if you just take your shoes off, you'll feel better right away."

"Hey!" David said. "It skipped our floor! We're going up."

Liz glanced up. The elevator was indeed going all the way up.

The elevator door opened, and Emma stepped in with a well-dressed redheaded girl.

"Adrienne?" Liz said, shocked. Liz looked at her friend. She couldn't believe her eyes. Adrienne had had a *serious* makeover. "You look incredible!" Liz said, giving Adrienne a hug. "When did you do this?"

"Last night." Adrienne smiled. "I got the Cameron Warner makeover at Bergdorf Goodman."

"You look amazing."

"She looks stupid," Emma said. "She looks like Cameron."

"Be nice," Liz warned Emma.

Emma shrugged and turned to Heather. The two girls stared each other down like cowboys in an old Western movie.

Liz rolled her eyes at Adrienne. The tension between the two little girls was funny.

"Wait a second," Liz said. "What are you doing here? Wasn't yesterday your last day?"

"Not quite." Adrienne laughed. "Mrs. Warner asked me to stay for another month. They couldn't get their nanny in time."

"That's great!" Liz cried. "But why didn't you call and tell me?"

Adrienne sighed. "I went out with Brian, and then I was up past midnight doing homework. Plus, my mother was not happy *at all* about the makeover."

"Why?" Liz asked.

"Beats me," Adrienne said. "She's so hypersensitive sometimes. She was furious about all the clothes. At first, she thought I'd spent all the money I'd earned on them. Then, when I explained that they were free, my mother went ballistic. I don't get it. I mean, what's the big deal?"

"They were free?" Liz said.

"Yeah. Cameron treated me. We even had personal shoppers—one for each of us."

"You had personal shoppers?"

"There's no other way to shop!" Adrienne replied. "Cameron's so great, don't you think?"

"I guess." Liz wasn't sure how she felt. She had really started to like Cameron at Mimi's. But the way she was now cozying up to Adrienne made Liz unsure. "It's kind of weird that Cameron just gave you all those clothes," Liz whispered, even though the kids didn't seem to be paying attention to their conversation. "I kind of see why your mom might be angry."

"It's not weird. She's my friend," Adrienne said. "And I can't believe you're siding with my mother!"

"I'm not. Okay . . . new subject," Liz said. She knew it was always better to stay away from the latest battle Adrienne was having with her mother. "Do you think Cameron will really set me up with Parker? I can't stop obsessing about it."

"You don't know? You're seeing Parker tonight!" Adrienne said as the elevator opened to Dr. M–C's apartment.

"Tonight? What are you talking about?" Liz demanded, holding open the elevator door with her foot.

"Oh, no!" Adrienne cried. "You don't know."

"Don't know what?"

"Cameron just told me upstairs that she's arranged a whole dinner party for us at Khmer, down on Bleecker Street. It's tonight! I'm bringing Brian, and she's making certain that Parker is there for you, and she invited some of her other friends from P–B also. We're meeting at eight-thirty."

I have a date with Parker! I have a date with Parker! Liz was finding it hard to breathe, she was so excited. It was at that moment that she caught a glance at her reflection in the mirror in Dr. M–C's entryway. She was wearing her school uniform. *There is no way I'm going on a date with the cutest guy in Manhattan wearing my school uniform!* she thought. *I have to go home to change.*

She looked at her watch and went over the different options in her mind. She had to work until eight tonight. She could race to the Upper West Side, change clothes, and then race all the way downtown. She knew she'd be really late. And she didn't trust that Parker would wait around for her. *I could borrow something out of Dr. M–C's closet,* she thought, *but she buys the worst things, and nothing would probably fit me.* She didn't dare ask Adrienne to swipe something from Mrs. Warner. That was way too risky if Cameron was coming to dinner.

"I'm going to have to run out and buy something to wear," Liz announced.

103

"I'll help you!" Heather shrieked. "I love to go shopping!"

"See," Adrienne said, pointing to Heather, "I told you there was nothing like a personal shopper!"

Oh, there is nothing here to wear! Liz thought, combing through the racks at Loehmann's, a discount store where she sometimes found great things very cheap.

Heather was in absolute heaven. She had never been in any store besides the children's department at Brooks Brothers, and for her, Loehmann's was a paradise of women's clothes and bustle. David, on the other hand, was beside himself with boredom. It was only through regular administrations of Halloween-sized Snickers bars that Liz managed to keep him under control.

"How about this?" Heather asked, pulling a vibrant Pucci knockoff off the rack.

"Too colorful," Liz said. "I need something really simple and sexy. Look for things in black."

Heather sorted through the racks. The two girls worked side by side until Liz felt she had seen everything in the huge store twice.

"Can we *please* go?" David begged. "I'm dying!"

Liz sighed. There was nothing.

"Okay. I give up," she said. "Let's go."

"Wait!" Heather cried. "What about this?"

"Never mind," Liz said. "Let's just . . ." Then she saw the dress in Heather's little hands.

It was perfect—a simple, little black dress in a fine wool crepe. It had a bateau neckline, and a tiny pink ribbon tied around its empire waist. It was Audrey Hepburn. It was Gwyneth Paltrow. Liz didn't care what it cost. She *had* to have it.

She turned to Heather. "Heather, you're the best!" She gave the girl a big hug. Heather beamed. Liz took the dress from Heather's hand. The tag had a bunch of prices and read: ORIGINALLY—$1,600; 50% OFF—$800; 50% OFF—$400; 50% OFF FINAL SALE—$200. The dress was still a little expensive, but Liz knew it would be worth it. She looked at the label. It was Oscar de la Renta. She had to try it on. She put the kids in two small chairs in the waiting room, and stood on a stool in her changing room so she could keep an eye on them, peering over the door as she dressed. *This must be what yoga is like,* she thought as she balanced on the teetering stool, pulled off her uniform cardigan, and stepped into the dress at the same time.

Exiting the dressing room, she turned to Heather and David. "What do we think?" she asked.

"You're pretty," David said, his mouth still covered with melted chocolate.

"Thanks." Liz smiled. "At least one guy today will think so."

On the way home, Liz called her mother. "Hi! Adrienne and I both just finished work, and we're heading to her apartment to watch a movie together. Can I sleep over?" Liz hated lying to her mother, but she knew her mother would never easily let her go downtown with a bunch of kids she didn't know. Ever since she was a little kid, her mom had to have a complete background check on anyone Liz wanted to hang out with. Liz didn't want to deal with explaining everything tonight.

"You can't sleep over," her mother said.

"Why not?" Liz tried to sound calm.

"We're leaving early tomorrow morning to go upstate to see your grandmother. Have fun with Adrienne, but make sure you're home by eleven. I'm going to wait up for you."

Liz knew there was no point arguing. Her parents were big on curfews. "All right. That's fine. Bye, Mom."

Eleven. If dinner was at eight-thirty, that was plenty of time to eat, flirt with Parker, and leave with him wanting more. *Cinderella timing*, she thought. *Arrive late, leave early. Make an impression.*

Liz finally put Heather and David to bed and hurried into the bathroom to change. Slipping on the new dress, she wished that she had a cashmere shawl or a little jacket that matched. Dr. M-C was out for the evening, and the housekeeper was in the kitchen watching TV.

It's just for one night, she thought, slipping into Dr. M-C's closet. She pulled a pale pink cashmere wrap from a shelf lined with dozens of shawls in every conceivable color. There wasn't a lot that Liz would ever want to wear in Dr. M-C's closet. Because of her size, most of her dresses looked like they had been made by some really expensive tent-maker, but her accessories were cool. She had more beautiful scarves and wraps than anyone Liz had ever known.

Sitting down at Dr. M-C's vanity, Liz used the mirror to quickly put on her makeup. The restaurant they were going to was very hip, so she paid special attention to her eyes, lining them in a smoky dark powder. A little gloss to the lips and she was done. She looked at herself in the mirror. Perfect. As a last touch, a spray of Joy—the most expensive perfume in the world and Dr. Markham-Collins's favorite. *Mine too,* Liz thought.

Liz shoved her school uniform in her backpack and grabbed a cab down to the restaurant. She would have to check her things at the door.

The bar at Khmer was packed with people and looked like a Vietnamese village. The tables were covered with grass umbrellas, and hidden lights gave an unearthly glow to the walls. The noise was overwhelming. The crowd was older. Much older.

Pulling her shawl a little bit tighter around her

shoulders, Liz forced her way through the crowd of people until she saw the others.

"I.D.?" a bouncer asked in a gruff voice.

Liz thought quickly. "I'm with Cameron Warner and Princess von Fallschirm," she said.

"Hey!" The guy gave her a big grin. "Any friend of Cam's and Mimi's gets right in. They're over there." He pointed to the bar where Adrienne, Cameron, Mimi, Graydon, Brian, and Parker sat with their drinks.

Brian saw her first. "Hey, Liz! You look great!"

"Thanks, Bri!" Liz gave Adrienne a hug and took in her outfit. It was very cool—a sexy, off-the-shoulder D&G top and a slim pair of Armani pants. Adrienne looked amazing, but something seemed wrong about the outfit. Then Liz realized what the problem was: Adrienne looked as if she were wearing a Cameron costume instead of her own clothes.

Cameron and Mimi waved to her, and Liz air-kissed them and then turned her attention to Parker.

"Hi," she said, "I'm Liz." She deliberately kept her voice soft so that Parker would have to lean closer to hear her and would get a little whiff of her perfume in the process. If there was anything Liz knew she did well, it was flirting without looking like she was flirting.

"I remember you," Parker said, smiling lazily at her. "I met you at Cam's last week."

"Oh, that's right!" Liz said, pretending she had forgotten. "How are you?"

"Better, now that you're here. I was asking Cam about you. I was hoping we could get together sometime soon."

Liz was stunned. *Could it be this easy? He's really interested!* Unsure of what to say, Liz gave him what she hoped was a mysterious smile.

"Okay, all of you, let's go downstairs! My other friends are at the table already," Cameron shouted above the din of the crowd. She carried her martini glass high over her head and stopped periodically so that people could take her picture.

Descending the staircase into Khmer's main dining room, Liz was amazed. Though the restaurant looked small from the street, there was a huge dining room belowground, complete with a soundproof lounge where people could dance. The room was full of a much older crowd, mostly in their twenties and thirties, and Liz was feeling a little out of place. Mimi and Cameron seemed to know everybody. Brian held Adrienne's hand and seemed surprisingly at home.

"Everyone," Cameron said, when they reached their table, "this is Bandar, and his friend Achim. Then we have Bibi, Kylie, and Tonia. Guys, this is everyone." She moved into the only logical place for her at the table: the head.

Parker came up behind Liz and, lightly touching her

shoulders, steered her to a seat, which he pulled out for her, and then gently sat her down. He took the seat next to her. "I've been looking forward to this," he said softly. "I wanted to get to know you better." He smiled at her.

He is so cute, Liz thought. *But he looks a little weird. It's his eyes,* Liz realized. They were red and kind of unfocused. *Maybe he's drunk,* Liz thought.

Parker looked at her again, and then reached into the basket on the table for an enormous piece of bread. "I love bread," Parker said. "Do you love bread, Liz?"

He's not drunk, Liz realized. *Parker is stoned.*

Liz was not into drugs, but she certainly knew enough people who got high. She hoped it wasn't a problem for him. Well, he hadn't seemed stoned the last time she'd seen him. *I'll just go with it and see what happens.*

"No, no, no!" Cameron said to Brian as he tried to sit next to Adrienne. "You *always* break up couples at a dinner party. Adrienne, you sit between Bandar and Achim, and Brian, you sit between me and Liz."

Bossy hostess though she was, Cameron soon had the table afire with conversation. Bandar bought horses for the Saudi royal family, and was totally fascinating, if, at thirty, too old and a bit oily. Achim was a cousin of Mimi's who had gone to school with Bandar in Switzerland. Bottle after bottle of champagne arrived at the table, and Liz was beginning to get a little nervous about splitting the bill when

Bandar announced that he hated the champagne they were drinking, and that he could never drink champagne at fifty dollars a bottle if there was something better to be had.

"So," he said, "since I do not feel I can force you all to pay for my extravagances, this whole dinner is on me." Everyone at the table cheered as Bandar called the waitress over and ordered different champagne. Liz caught Adrienne's eye across the table, and both girls smiled at each other, totally relieved. Adrienne leaned over and whispered to Liz, "Did you get carded at the door?"

"No. I said I was with Cameron and Mimi."

"Us, too."

"Money must take care of everything!" Liz grinned. She turned back to Parker. "That's very nice of Bandar, isn't it?" she said.

"Actually," Parker said, "though I'm happy to drink his champagne, I think he's kind of an asshole."

Liz giggled. "Why do you say that? He seems perfectly nice, to me."

Parker looked her right in the eyes. "Liz, what kind of guy takes seven kids in high school out for an expensive dinner? He's thirty."

Parker's right, Liz thought. *It's totally creepy.*

Liz and Parker talked some more. The more champagne Liz drank, the better and better Parker looked and sounded. He leaned closer toward her, put his hand on her knee, and the room seemed to melt away.

Oh. Hold on. Going too fast. Gotta talk to Adrienne, a voice inside her head said suddenly. She made eye contact with Adrienne and pointed toward the restrooms. The two girls got up and left.

"This place is so cool," Adrienne said, once inside. "Did you see that the table next to us has Tyra Banks and that girl who won *American Idol?*" Adrienne seemed a little overwhelmed. This was not Van Rensselaer.

"I know." Liz smiled. "And Parker is the best." The two girls screamed and jumped up and down for a second, until an older woman walked into the women's room. The two girls attempted to look cool.

"I'm so happy for you!" Adrienne said, and reapplied some lip gloss. "Don't you think that Bandar is hilarious?" She shook out her new hairstyle.

"I'd watch out for him," Liz said. "I mean, what kind of guy takes out high school kids for dinner?"

"He's a friend of Mimi's cousin. I think he's cool," Adrienne said defiantly. "His best friend is a Saudi prince. I don't think we are in a position to refuse his hospitality," she said loftily.

Liz smiled. Adrienne was obviously repeating something that Cameron had said. She never would have come up with that on her own. "Adrienne, you're starting to sound a lot like Cameron."

"I'm learning a lot from Cam."

"Oh, so now suddenly she's 'Cam' to you?"

"Come on, Liz! I'm having fun, and so are you. Parker looks like he's really into you."

"I think he is," Liz confided. "Listen, we'd better go back outside."

The two girls made their way through the crowded room. They ate the amazing dinner that Bandar ordered, and drank bottle after bottle of the incredible champagne. Aside from Tonia calling Bandar 'Band-Aid' by mistake, everything went really well.

Wow, Liz thought, *I've had a lot more to drink than I thought. I'm pretty bombed.* She looked next to her at Brian. He was staring at Cameron, who was staring back at him intently.

"I know you must be a big music fan."

"I am," he said. "I go to a lot of concerts."

"But have you ever been to a concert at Madison Square Garden in a corporate skybox with backstage passes?" Cameron asked huskily. She reached over deliberately and put her hand on his arm.

"No way!" he said, laughing. "I can't afford those!"

"It's the only way to see a concert. Trust me," she said, looking into his eyes.

"Oh, I trust you all right," Brian said, laughing. "I'm sure it is."

"So," Cameron said, leaning closer and closer. "If you trust me, how about joining me on Saturday night at Madison Square Garden for the Radiohead concert?"

"Are you serious? You can get tickets to that?"

"Brian doesn't really like Radiohead," Liz said suddenly.

"I do, too," Brian said, looking surprised.

"I thought so," Cameron said. "In fact, I have the tickets already." She smiled the sweetest of smiles.

Liz stared at the two of them, and then glanced at Adrienne. Did she see what just happened? No. Adrienne was listening to Bandar's boring stories about his high school in Switzerland.

Liz glanced at her watch. It was almost eleven. She was buzzed, and she had to go. She turned to Brian. "Hey, Brian, I have got to go. I have a curfew. Do you and Adrienne want to go with me?" She hoped he would. She didn't want Cameron to get her claws into Brian any further than she already had.

"Curfew?" Cameron shrieked. "Liz, that is so cute! You guys! Liz has a curfew!"

There she is, thought Liz. *That's the Cameron Warner I know.*

"That was pretty bitchy," Parker whispered. "I'm sorry. Can I put you in a cab?"

"That would be really nice, Parker. Thanks." Liz gave him a big smile. "Are you coming, guys?"

"I'm going to stay," Brian said. "I can take the express to Washington Heights."

"Well, aren't you sweet!" Cameron said, and kissed Brian on the cheek.

Liz moved over to Adrienne and pulled her away from Bandar. "Adrienne, I have to go. It's getting late."

"I'm so glad you came!" Adrienne said, obviously having had too much of Bandar's champagne.

"No, Adrienne, seriously. I'd watch Cameron. She's had too much to drink, and she's all over Brian."

"She's so nice!" Adrienne said, pushing Liz away.

"Adrienne!" Liz whispered. "I think you should take Brian home—now!"

Adrienne looked at her friend and focused. "Okay," she said, "I get the message. Thanks. You okay by yourself?"

"I'm okay," Liz said, nodding toward Parker. "Talk to you tomorrow."

Parker walked Liz upstairs, out of the busy restaurant and onto the quiet, darkened streets of Greenwich Village.

"I love it downtown," Liz said, as they passed the Magnolia Bakery and the Mark Jacobs store.

"Me, too. It's so quiet and charming here. Hey, you want to split a cupcake?"

Liz looked at her watch. Eleven. Pumpkin time. "I wish I could. I have to get home, though."

"No problem. Rain check." He raised his arm, and

hailed a cab heading up Hudson Street. Liz was about to slide in when Parker took her by the waist and gave her a kiss.

Parker's warm hands moved up and down her back. His tongue gently explored her mouth, and he breathed softly, pulling her closer to him. He ran his fingers up and down her bare arms, and her whole body burst into goose bumps.

Now that was a really good kiss, she thought.

"I think I wanted that a lot more than a cupcake," he said. "See you."

"Bye," Liz said, for the lack of anything better.

The cab sped up the West Side Highway, and Liz looked out over the glittering Hudson River and the breathtakingly tall new apartment buildings. The city was beautiful. She thought of gorgeous Parker and the kiss. Tonight, *everything* was beautiful.

CHAPTER TEN

dazzled

Wednesday afternoon at school, Adrienne texted Brian for the third time.

Where is he? she wondered. *It never takes this long to hear from him.* She stared at her phone, silently willing him to text her back. Maybe his cell was out of juice or something.

"Hey!" Tamara said, coming up behind her. "Girl, you look terrible! Are you sick or something?"

"Not exactly," Adrienne said. "A little stressed. I have a world history test next period. And Brian is not texting me back."

"Where is he?" Tamara asked. "Why wasn't he in class today?"

"He wasn't in class today?" Adrienne said. Brian had *never* missed a day of school before—he was obsessed with being there every day. His older brother, Jimmy, had had a perfect attendance record in high school, and Brian was trying for one, too. It had never even occurred to her that he might not even be in the building.

"No. He didn't show, and he missed the serious study session for Monday's physics test," Tamara said. "He would be toast, if only . . ."

"If only what?" Adrienne asked.

"If only *I* hadn't made a copy of my perfectly taken physics notes for him." Tamara smiled and handed over the pages to Adrienne. "You tell Brian he *owes* me one. And, the two of you can pay me back by making sure you come to my birthday on Saturday. No excuses, okay? We are going to get *down* at this little joint in Williamsburg. It is a Brooklyn party, Adrienne—leave the Prada at home!" She laughed and gave Adrienne a quick hug. "I'm serious. You've been hanging with those Fifth Avenue bitches too long." Tamara stopped. "Sorry. I care about you. Anyway, give those notes to Brian when you see him and, remember, I'll see you on Saturday—or else!" Tamara took off down the hall as the next bell rang.

Adrienne pressed her head against her locker. She took a deep breath. Something was wrong. She didn't know how she knew—she just felt it. She had to talk to Liz.

Adrienne pulled out her phone and texted her friend.

BRI MIA ????

Within seconds, the phone rang. It was Liz.

"Hey!" she said. "What's up? Where's Brian?"

"I don't know. He's not in school. I'm starting to freak a little."

"Are you sure nothing happened Friday night after I left?" Liz asked.

"Nothing. I told you—we hung out for a while, and then Brian and I went home."

"I still think something was going on between Brian and Cam," Liz said.

"Liz, nothing was going on. Brian and I are fine. You may not trust Cameron, but I *do* trust Brian. Anything happening with Parker?"

"No," Liz said, "He hasn't called me. Is that weird? Should I think that's weird? I was thinking about calling him . . . but then I think no—right?"

"I don't know—"

"Listen, I have to go. The bell's ringing. I have class. Don't worry. Brian's probably under the covers at home, sick or something. Later!" She hung up.

Adrienne smiled. Liz was probably right. *Brian's probably fine. It's nothing to stress about.*

At the end of the day, Brian finally showed up at school, sliding into his seat in English class between Adrienne and Tamara.

"Where have you been?" Adrienne whispered to him. "I was worried about you." She slid him Tamara's notes.

"You'll never believe where I was. I was on my way to school, and I get this call from Cameron."

Adrienne stopped smiling. Friday night at Khmer, she had noticed that Cameron was too friendly, but she had decided not to make a big deal about it. She trusted Brian, but this was way different. Cam should know better—calling another girl's boyfriend was *not done*.

"And . . . ," Adrienne said.

"Yeah, and?" Tamara said, leaning forward.

"So, Cam calls, and says she's cutting school today because her dad got her into a recording studio in Midtown to watch P. Diddy lay down the final tracks for his album."

"So?" Adrienne said. "Cam can afford to skip school. She doesn't need the grades. We do."

"That's right," Tamara said. "But P. Diddy? That is so cool!"

"I know it!" he said sheepishly. "I couldn't pass it up, so Cam and I went. It was AMAZING. We met Jay-Z and Beyoncé. Cam knew everybody. It was like *her* party! And they had all this food, and everyone was hanging out and dancing, and I just had to stay."

"Jay-Z?" Tamara said. "Really?"

"Really," Brian said.

"Well," Adrienne said. She knew her voice sounded strange—too high-pitched. "I'm glad that you had such an amazing time."

She couldn't believe it. Brian of all people—her down-to-earth boyfriend—was dazzled by the money, caught up in the world of the megarich. The idea of it almost made her laugh, until the reality of what was happening hit her: Brian wasn't dazzled by the money. Brian was dazzled by Cameron.

Was Cameron trying to steal her boyfriend?

Liz was almost finished with school on Thursday, when her phone rang. *Adrienne, I bet. I wonder what's happening with Brian.*

Luckily, Liz was in art class and the teacher was pretty laid back. She walked over to the sink and pretended to wash her paintbrush while quietly answering her phone.

"Elizabeth?" Dr. M-C boomed. "Where are you?"

"I'm at school, Dr. Markham-Collins. I'll be there in an hour or so."

"No, Elizabeth, I need you right *now*. You'll see why when you get here. Please hurry." She hung up.

I am so busted, Liz thought. *I bet she noticed the missing shawl. Well, at least I only have gym left—I can cut that easily. Why did I take that stupid shawl . . . ?*

The service elevator opened into Dr. M-C's kitchen. The first sound that greeted Liz was the buzz of an electric saw and hammering. Heather was sitting in a chair in the kitchen with her hands over her ears, and David was lying on the floor, moaning.

"Liz, make them stop! All the noise is shattering my nerves!" Heather whined.

"David, get up off the floor! What's going on?"

"They are tearing things up! For the magazine," David said. "Ow, my stomach hurts from your little cakes."

"My what?" Liz asked.

"You got a package, and David opened it. I hid it so he wouldn't get in trouble with Mommy," Heather said.

"Where is it?" Liz asked.

Heather went to a cabinet and pulled out a large white box. A card was attached: *Can't stop thinking about you. I thought a dozen roses would be lame. Parker*

Liz smiled and opened the box. Inside were what appeared to be the remains of a dozen cupcakes from the Magnolia Bakery. "Oh, no," Liz said. "David, you didn't eat all of these, did you?"

"Mommy picked us up from school early. She said she might need us for pictures, and then she said we couldn't leave the kitchen. There was no lunch, only soy nuggets. The cupcakes came. They smelled good. . . ."

"I had one," Heather said. "Only one! I was good."

"Oh, it's okay," Liz said. *I sure hope he doesn't puke,* she thought as David clutched his stomach. "Listen," she said, "let's get in there and see what's going on."

Entering what had once been the dining room, Liz looked around in horror.

The ceiling was gone. The walls between the dining room and the library had been torn down and replaced by support columns. The hall had been completely destroyed. The mirrors that had formerly hidden Dr. Markham-Collins's office had been torn down. Her private office was revealed to be a pretty small and uninteresting place.

"Liz!" Dr. M-C hollered over the roar of power saws. "Can you believe it? Two hours, and the whole apartment reduced to a shambles!" She introduced a middle-aged woman in a Jil Sander suit and high heels. "This is Darby DuPlane, my new interior designer. Darby, this is my nanny, Liz."

Thank God this isn't about the shawl, Liz thought.

"Liz, come on over," Darby said. "I want to show you what we're doing." Darby grabbed Liz around the shoulders, pulling Heather and David from her hands. The children stood, alone and nervous, in the wreckage that had been their home.

"I went through the house with a marketing analyst. The apartment was too cold. Too impersonal. Not child-friendly. It was just not the home of a woman who needs to be perceived as a quote GREAT MOM." Darby made quotation gestures with her fingers. "So . . . out with the Donghia and pale gray 'don't touch me, please' suede, and contemporary art, and in with . . ." She pulled a sheet off an easel, revealing renderings of what the new interior of the apartment would look like.

Liz knew that she knew nothing about interior design, but she thought Darby DuPlane's plan, well, kind of sucked.

The apartment looked like it was going to be a Disney version of the lobby of a big hotel. Huge, over-upholstered sofas in vibrant chintzes, potted palms, and illustrations from famous children's books all over the walls.

"This apartment will say, 'I'm accessible. I love kids. I have no secrets,'" Darby explained.

This apartment will say, "I have no taste at all," Liz thought. *What is she thinking?*

"Darby bought the illustrations from *The Cat in the Hat* and *Green Eggs and Ham*," Dr. M-C added. "It will be amazing."

"And no hiding behind mirrors," Darby said, wagging her finger at Dr. M-C.

"No," Dr. M-C agreed. "So hostile."

"Well, it looks incredible," Liz said. "Why don't I go back into the kitchen with the kids?" she suggested as a hunk of plaster crashed to the floor, showering them all with dust.

Heather began to wheeze.

"Good idea. Take them back to the kitchen," Dr.

Markham-Collins said, never even acknowledging her own children.

"Mayra, get them *out* of the apartment!" Darby said. "Children need some air!"

"Liz, could you?" Dr. Markham-Collins asked.

"Sure thing," Liz said.

"Oh. And don't touch anything in the kitchen, and I mean *anything*. It's *photo-ready*, and it needs to be shot for *New York* magazine this weekend. And by that, I mean yesterday, if you know what I mean!" She and Darby laughed as they left the room.

"I'm scared," Heather said, picking at her hair.

"My stomach hurts," David said for the thirtieth time.

"I totally understand." Liz peered quizzically at Heather. "Heather, why are you pulling at your hair?"

"Something is stuck in it. Like a rubber band. Or something."

"Did you put a rubber band in your hair?" Liz asked.

"No," Heather said.

"Let me see." Liz pulled Heather's head toward her.

Liz quickly discovered that the thing in Heather's hair was gum.

"Heather, were you chewing gum today?" Liz asked.

"No!" Heather screamed, quickly becoming hysterical. "David threw gum at me at school. He did it! HE DID IT!"

The two children quickly became screaming, crying, fighting messes, rolling around on the floor.

"Stop it!" Liz yelled, totally losing her cool. "Heather, get off your brother! David, I am telling you right now that we need a serious, major time-out!"

"We can't have a time-out," Heather said. "Our rooms are gone."

Liz reached into her bag and pulled out her cell phone. There was only one person in the world who could help.

Liz called her mother.

"Hi, honey! How's your day?"

"Later, Mom, later. I have an eight-year-old with gum in her hair, and a five-year-old who has eaten close to a dozen cupcakes. What should I do?"

There was a chuckle on the other end of the phone.

Liz was furious. Her mother was laughing at her!

"I'm sorry! It's just funny . . ."

Yeah. Funny, she thought.

"Mom!" Liz could hear herself start to whine.

"I'm sorry. Okay. Listen. The gum. Get some peanut butter and rub it in. The peanut oil loosens the gum. As for the cupcake kid . . . " Mrs. Braun began to giggle again.

Liz waited. This was *so* demeaning.

"Sorry. Now you know what it's like for me. Well, he'll either feel better, or he'll throw up. There's nothing you can do. It sounds absolutely dreadful, sweetheart. Do you want me to stay on the line while you try the peanut butter?"

"No, Mom, it's okay. I think I've got it. Thanks." Liz hung up.

Peanut butter.

Liz searched the kitchen. Finally she found peanut butter. Unfortunately, it was the organic kind.

"Let's give this a shot, Heather," Liz said kindly, working the peanut butter into the tangle and massaging it gently.

"That stinks!" Heather wailed. "And it hurts!"

"The gum will come out. I promise!" Liz insisted, glancing at the green-looking David.

"It won't!" Heather wailed. "You'll have to shave me bald!"

Liz glanced back at David, who was rolling on the floor. She prayed he wouldn't throw up in the photo-ready kitchen of Ms. Darby DuPlane.

Liz rubbed Heather's hair. The peanut butter wasn't working. The gum was stuck. Suddenly the door to the kitchen opened. Liz whirled around, covered in peanut butter, cupcake crumbs, and plaster dust.

"Well, you're a mess," said a familiar voice. "Is this how you look during the day?"

It was Parker. Parker!!

Could this day get worse? Liz asked herself.

"What are you doing here?" she asked. *Is there anywhere I can hide?*

Smiling his killer smile, Parker walked closer. "I came to see if you got my cupcakes," he said. "Cameron said you were down here, and I thought I'd visit. I wanted to see you again before I took off."

Cameron! Liz sighed. *Of course, it wouldn't occur to her that I'm working!*

"I'm covered in peanut butter," Liz said helplessly, for lack of anything better to say.

"I love peanut butter," Parker said with a grin.

"Who is he?" Heather demanded.

"Now I'm really going to be sick," David said, pressing his face against the cool tile floor of the kitchen.

"Wait," Liz said. "Take off for where?"

Parker smiled. "This weekend is when we all open our houses in Palm Beach. No one will be in New York this weekend. The Warners, the von Fallschirms, my family. We all take off *tonight*." He grinned. "Can we go out next week? Just you and me?"

"Sure," Liz said, and grinned.

Parker smiled again. "You are cute."

Despite Heather's whining and moaning, the gum miraculously loosened, and Heather cheered up. "I won't have to be bald?" she asked.

"No, Heather, you won't have to be bald," Liz said.

Just then, Dr. Markham-Collins entered the kitchen with Darby, her new evil sidekick. "Who's going to be bald?" she asked, confused. "Elizabeth! Heather looks like a sandwich. What on earth is going on?" Walking farther into the kitchen, she noticed Parker. "And who are you?" she asked. "Again, Elizabeth, these constant unapproved guests! What can I say . . ." She raised her hands in a gesture of despair.

"Dr. Markham-Collins, what a pleasure to finally meet you," Parker said, turning on his megawatt smile and his charm. "I'm Parker Devlin, Reed and Lauren Devlin's son."

Dr. Markham-Collins became a mass of social-climbing jelly. "Oh, Parker, how lovely to meet you!" she trilled. "Your father is a captain of industry, *so* important, *such* a philanthropist. Such a *leader*." She smiled. "What are you doing here?" she asked, seeming confused. She glanced around the apartment as if she was expecting Cameron or Mimi to be with the well-connected Parker.

"Well, Liz . . . whom I'm dating," he said, looking at Liz with a shy little glance, "has told me how great your kids are, and I would love to take them all to the museum. You obviously need a little space right now. Why don't I take them all out for a couple of hours, give them some-thing to eat in the patron's dining room, and get everyone out of your hair?"

"*You* are dating Liz?" Dr. Markham-Collins asked incredulously. Then she suddenly caught herself. "Parker," she continued, "you are, I think, an *angel* sent to me and my children. And Liz is *lucky*. Thank you so much. Please tell your father that—"

Before Liz knew it, in a flurry of thanks, Parker had whisked all of them into the waiting elevator and out of the building.

The four of them trudged along Fifth Avenue in silence, when suddenly, and for the first time in Liz's memory, Heather Markham-Collins began to laugh.

"I'm sorry!" she said, trying to stop. "Mommy was so funny! 'Your father is a *captain*!'" she said, in perfect imitation of her mother. Her giggles grew into a huge, aching belly laugh. A laugh so infectious, it made David laugh, too. Before they both knew it, Parker and Liz were laughing, and the four of them walked into the Metropolitan Museum of Art covered with dust and laughing themselves silly.

Parker was an amazing guide.

The Metropolitan was like a playground. He showed Heather the rooms of French furniture that had belonged to princesses and queens, and he took David to see the Greek and Roman warriors and the Hall of Armor. They ran through the Costume Institute, and the halls of ancient

Chinese art, stopping in Astor Court to rest for a bit amid the gurgling of the pool where the golden fish made kissing faces at them.

Finally, they made their way into the Egyptian rooms and the Temple of Dendur.

Standing in front of the Temple—a whole building removed from Egypt and rebuilt inside the Met—Liz looked at Parker. *He's amazing,* she thought. *And he really likes me.*

At that moment, Parker took her in his arms and kissed her. This time, she kissed him hard. His lips were strong and soft at the same time, and his hands pulled her closer to him.

The setting sun flooded the galleries, and a feeling of warmth ran through Liz's body, thrilling her from her head to her feet—her feet which suddenly felt too warm and too wet.

Liz broke away and looked down. She was standing in a puddle of what had once been a dozen cupcakes from the Magnolia Bakery.

"I told you I felt sick," David said.

CHAPTER ELEVEN

bomb ditch

The next afternoon, up in the penthouse at 841 Fifth Avenue, Adrienne was met with the most amazing spectacle: The entire dining room and front hallway were filled with hundreds of suitcases and trunks labeled with colored identification tags. The place looked like the luggage terminal at Kennedy Airport. Tania, with a clipboard in her hands, was racing around the place, shouting out instructions in her exceptionally bizarre English.

"What is all this?" Adrienne asked Tania, catching her by the arm.

"Bomb Ditch," Tania replied.

"What?" Adrienne asked.

Tania sighed, completely exasperated. "To Floridoo. Bomb Ditch, where Warners in estates."

Adrienne thought for a second, trying to pierce the enigma of Tania's English. "Oh!" Adrienne called out. "Palm Beach in Florida!"

"Is what I am say," Tania replied. "Bomb Ditch. Very busy. You must to make Miss Emma pack."

"Thank God you're here, Adriana!" Mrs. Warner called out. She entered the hall, preceeded by a cloud of her perfume and trailed by her personal assistant, a thin, nervous woman. Adrienne couldn't remember this one's name. The only thing Mrs. Warner went through faster than nannies were personal assistants.

Taking a deep breath, Adrienne decided to stand up for herself. "Adrienne," she said clearly. "My name is Adrienne."

"How terrible. You should change it. Adriana has a bit of chic to it. Now, where are your bags?"

"My bags?" Adrienne asked, incredulous. *Do we even speak the same language?* she wondered.

"Well, darling, you don't think you can get through opening weekend in Palm Beach on one outfit, do you? I mean, I suppose you and Cameron could hit Worth Avenue and the Via Mizner, but the clothes there are so overpriced. Anyway, you don't think that we could open the house without having someone to watch Emma, do you? She could drown in the pool or on the beach. Darling, she might even get lost in the *house,* for God's sake." With that, Mrs. Warner trailed out of the hall, throwing instructions into the air behind her like rice at a wedding. Her beleaguered personal assistant trailed behind her, taking notes.

Emma wandered in, looking pale and lost. Catching sight of Adrienne, she ran up. "Are you really coming to Palm Beach?"

"Well, no one told me I was supposed to, and I can't. I have, um, plans this weekend," Adrienne said to Emma. "Emma, you look upset. Is everything okay?"

"I hate Palm Beach," Emma said simply. "As soon as we get there, everyone forgets about me. I get really lonely there. We only have satellite TV. And a pool. And a bowling alley. And a private beach. Sure you can't come?"

"It doesn't sound bad," Adrienne said, "but no, I can't."

Emma sighed in impatience. "Adrienne, you don't get it. There is no *Oprah* on the weekends in Palm Beach. I have nothing to do."

Adrienne smiled at Emma. Palm Beach. It was very tempting. If only.

"Emma, I really can't. Last week I went out with Cam and her friends and I got home really late. My mom is really angry at me, and I just can't go to Florida."

"Of course you can!" said a cheerful voice behind her. "Florida is the best!"

Adrienne turned to see Cameron walk in. She looked radiant. It was nauseating. Her skin and eyes were clear, her hair was freshly blown out, and she was already wearing summer clothes and a tan. *It is so unfair,* Adrienne thought. *It's like she has a pact with Satan.*

"Hey!" Cameron continued cheerfully. "Did your boyfriend tell you what we did on Wednesday?"

Adrienne decided to lay down the law, right then and there.

"Well, Cam, it's just that . . . " Adrienne took a deep breath. "It's just, you know, Brian isn't from your world, and he's a little taken in by all the glamour and the invitations—you know? And well, I'd hate for him to get the idea that you are trying to get together with him . . . or something."

Cameron looked at her with a bemused expression. "Are you done?" she asked.

"Yeah," Adrienne admitted.

"Adrienne, I am not saying this to hurt your feelings. I'm just telling you the truth, and I don't want to sound mean. But seriously, I am *not* interested in Brian."

"But Cameron, you—" Adrienne interrupted.

"Adrienne," Cameron said firmly, suddenly sounding angry. "Do you really think that a girl like me would try to steal a broke, seventeen-year-old boy who goes to a public school from a girlfriend who works as her family's nanny? Adrienne, you're a smart girl—do you really think that I'd waste my time trying to steal Brian? I like you guys. You're both real. I took Brian to the recording session for the same reason I took you to Bergdorf's. It was fun for me to watch you two have a good time. Chill, sweetie. Please. Let's not get ugly over nothing."

135

Adrienne took another deep breath. Cam was totally right. She had nothing to worry about. "Cool," she said. "As long as we're clear."

"Crystal," Cameron said. "So Palm Beach is heaven right now. It used to be so old-people's-home, but now, West Palm is totally happening, and you can't beat our house. It makes this apartment look like a tenement."

"Really?" Adrienne said, interested.

"You've got to come. Palm Beach is an island off the coast of Florida. Lake Worth separates Palm Beach from West Palm. The best houses are on the ocean, and the other great houses are on Lake Worth. Our house"—she paused dramatically—"is on both. It goes right through the whole of Palm Beach. My parents stay in the Villa on the ocean, and we stay in the Lake House, which is so far away, we can do whatever we want without getting caught."

Cameron and a whole house of her own in the sun down in Florida. It sounded like heaven. But, no. Her parents would never let her.

"Cameron, my mom is on the warpath. When I got home from Khmer, she was furious. She grounded me. Believe me, she's not letting me go to Florida with you."

The smile fell from Cameron's face. "Adrienne, I'm serious now. You have to come to Florida with us. If you don't go, my stepmother will fire you."

Adrienne swallowed. She certainly didn't want that.

136

"Don't worry. My stepmother will call your mom. I guarantee you're coming. No one says 'no' to Christine Olivia Warner. If she wants you in Florida, you'll be in Florida."

"What about the plane ticket?" Adrienne asked. "Will your parents buy one for me?"

Cameron looked at her in shock. "Adrienne," Cameron purred. "What ticket? We have our own plane!"

CHAPTER TWELVE

in the hot tub—naked

The private plane was incredible. The walls were covered in silk brocade, and the elaborately upholstered chairs looked like the ones in the Warners' living room but were bolted to the floor and had seatbelts. There were two flight attendants who spent most of their time delivering drinks to Mr. Warner, who stayed glued to his wireless computer and telephone headset for most of the flight.

Adrienne had never seen Mr. Warner before, and she checked him out with interest. He was in his late fifties or maybe even a bit older, but he was handsome, with chiseled good looks and a deep tan. His eyes were steely and focused as he did his work. As the drinks were delivered during the flight, however, he paid less and less attention to the computer and more and more attention to the attractive attendants. An hour after takeoff, he was asleep.

Some "love match," Adrienne thought, glancing at Mrs. Warner buried behind a *Town and Country* magazine.

They don't even look at each other.

Graydon Warner had already spent most of the flight leering at her, which grossed Adrienne out. She turned to Cameron to avoid having to speak to Graydon. "I can't believe there's a piano on your plane!" Adrienne exclaimed. She pointed to the miniature piano for Emma to practice on.

"The piano was made by Thomas Chickering of Boston in 1850 for his daughter," Cameron informed Adrienne. "But Emma won't play it. She thinks it stinks."

"Shut up, Cam!" Emma, in a rare eight-year-old gesture, stuck her tongue out at Cameron and made a face.

"The least you can do is play it. Dad paid a half a million for it just to please you," Cameron said.

Emma stood, marched over to the piano and, without hesitation, pounded out Elton John's "The Bitch is Back."

"Very funny, Rumpelstiltskin," Cameron said, sticking out her foot and kicking Emma in the ankle.

"Hey, girls, break it up!" Adrienne said, pulling Emma out of Cameron's reach, which was difficult. Cam's legs were so long, she could probably have kicked the pilot from her seat.

Cameron sighed. "I'd appreciate it if you'd keep the monster under control, Adrienne. Some of us would like to rest just a *little* before the plane lands." She turned her chair away from Adrienne, put on her sunglasses, and pulled a Hermès lap blanket up over her bare legs.

After a few hours, the plane landed on the private runway of the West Palm Beach International Airport. The front door opened to reveal a staircase that had been rolled up so they could exit. The family filed out of the plane, and Adrienne stood, smelling the humid, rich air. The sun had already set.

Two huge white Rolls-Royces pulled up in front of the plane.

"Normally," said Cameron, walking down the staircase like a showgirl in Vegas, "white cars are tacky. In Palm Beach, they're de rigueur. Can you imagine a black car in this heat?"

"That means they're *necessary*," Emma added.

"I know," Adrienne said, poking Emma, and tripping slightly as she stepped off the stairs and onto the tarmac.

"See you at the house," Cameron said. "The first car is for my parents, me, and Graydon. The second car is for you and Emma. The minivan is for the rest of the servants, and the trucks are for the luggage." Adrienne blinked. There was a convoy of vehicles on the tarmac, all for the Warners.

Emma and Adrienne got into the car, which was spacious and cool. Not, however, as cool as Emma was being.

"Emma, hey, what's the matter?" Adrienne prodded.

"You like Cameron better than you like me."

"That's not true. Listen," Adrienne said, putting her arm around Emma, surprised that Emma let it stay there.

"Cam and I are the same age. We're friends. I like you a lot, and I hope you like me. I'm not less of a friend to you because I'm Cameron's friend, too."

"Cameron has no friends," Emma said sharply. "Don't let her fool you."

"Cameron's not fooling me," Adrienne said.

"Yes, she is," Emma said, staring Adrienne in the face. "I just hope that you are going to have some time for me this weekend."

"Emma," Adrienne replied, "I'm only down here because of you. What else would I do in Florida but hang out with you?"

They drove along the ocean, and finally arrived at La Villa Manon, pulling in through the massive wrought-iron gates. The car wound through brightly lit paths lined with coconut palms and innumerable hibiscus and gardenia bushes, which left a heavy perfume hanging in the air. Enormous volcanic rocks had rare orchids growing out of them, and orange trees in tubs covered the terraces of the house, which suddenly appeared before them at the end of a vast expanse of perfect green lawn.

The house was Spanish in style, painted a delicate shell-pink. It had a tiled roof and covered balconies. It looked, Adrienne thought, about the size of the airport they had left. There were colonnades and terraces made of black-flecked white travertine marble, and fountains everywhere. Every room on the second floor had a balcony overlooking the sea, and the French doors on the first floor were all wide open to receive the breezes from the Atlantic Ocean.

The car drove into the cobbled courtyard, and Emma pulled Adrienne inside.

The house was like a palace in Europe or a movie star's home in Hollywood. Everywhere Adrienne looked there were incredible paintings and furniture, flowers, and precious things. There was even a collection of jewel-studded shells lying on a table, as if they had been pulled off the beach. *That is,* Adrienne thought, *if there were a beach where you could pick up a diamond-and-sapphire-encrusted conch shell!*

"Let's go down to the Lake House!" Emma said, running ahead of Adrienne through the doors into what must, Adrienne thought, be a ballroom. The enormous room with crystal chandelier faced a huge lawn that swept down to a little version of the main house. A cascade of lit fountains lined the pathway. Beyond the Lake House were the private boat docks in Lake Worth, and a view of the coast of West Palm Beach, twinkling in the distance.

Entering the Lake House, Adrienne could see that Tania was already busy unpacking Emma's things.

"You go upstairs to your rooms!" Tania said. "Miss Cameron, she send you packings!"

What on earth does that mean? Adrienne wondered.

142

"Emma," Adrienne asked, "is it okay if I go to my room for a little while?"

"Sure," Emma said. "See you later."

Adrienne climbed the stairs. The walls were of tinted plaster, polished so highly that they looked like they were made of marble. Pieces of porcelain painted with pictures of tropical plants were hung on the walls like art. The porcelain was beautiful, as were all the gold lighting fixtures. *All this in a house where children and servants stay, that guests don't even see!* she thought.

She finally found a door with a small sign on it that read, MISS LEWIS, NANNY.

Entering her room, Adrienne was thrilled. Twice the size of her room at home, it had pretty flowered wallpaper and a canopy bed, hung with pink and white silk gingham curtains. The carpet was pale green with a trellis pattern, and there were several pretty pieces of furniture painted to look like bamboo.

I think I'm going to love Florida! Adrienne thought, walking over to the shutters, which hid the view. Adrienne grinned. *Ocean or lake?* she wondered.

Opening the shutters, she was disappointed. "Parking lot," she said. Her view was of the service lot and several large air-conditioning units that hummed and growled. A large emergency electrical generator made puffs of smoke, which drifted up to her open window.

Maybe I'll just keep these shutters closed, she thought. She went to the closet, opened it, and gasped. It was filled with fabulous clothes and a note for Adrienne from Cameron.

This was all mine last season. You can totally wear them— half of it I never even used. I'll see you tonight at eleven at the pool of this house—I'm in "the Big House" with my parents. Can you make sure that by eleven there is food and liquor downstairs at the pool? We are having a party! Lots of Palm Beach friends—so make sure there is plenty of booze. Hector will help you. Thanks! Cam. P.S. Remember to keep it a secret—my parents can't know!

Oh, no, Adrienne thought, panic quickly setting in. *She wants me to pull together a party? I don't know how to do anything here. Who knows what these kids from Palm Beach will expect?*

Adrienne sighed and stared at the note. *And who in the world is Hector?* she wondered.

———

By 9:45, Adrienne was in a frenzy. When she tried to get things from the kitchen, she discovered that she wasn't allowed to order food or drinks without Tania's permission. Tania was happy to let her order a snack, even though she had eaten dinner earlier with Emma, but there was no way she could order alcohol or enough food for every one Cameron was probably inviting. *Not that I have any idea how many people that even is,* Adrienne realized.

She went out to the pool and looked at the note

again. Hector. She had to find Hector. Then she noticed a really handsome Latin guy cleaning the pool and lighting the tiki torches. "Hi!" she called. "Are you Hector?"

"Who wants to know?" he asked.

"I'm Adrienne, Emma's nanny," she said.

"And a very pretty nanny you are, too!" he said, throwing his cigarette into the bushes and walking toward her. "How can I help you?"

"Cameron said—" Adrienne began.

"That I could help you set up for a party, right?" He shook his head. "Not a lot of time, right? You should have come earlier." He made her feel stupid.

"I got stuck with Emma and her dinner," Adrienne explained, not really sure why she was making excuses to him. *He can't be that much older than I am, and he is cleaning pools, after all,* she thought.

"Okay. Give me five," he said.

"Five what?" she asked. "Five minutes?"

"No. Five hundred dollars," he said. "You see, I have to break into the Warners' liquor storage room, and then take a boat to West Palm to pick up food and mixers. It's not easy."

"Cameron didn't give me any money. I don't have five hundred," Adrienne admitted. *Break into the liquor storage room? How much trouble am I going to get into?*

"I know you're good for it," he said. "The Warners

will pay you for the whole weekend tomorrow, and I'll come get it from you. *You* can get the cash from Cameron later. I only deal with the nanny. Cameron is too good to talk to me herself," he said with disgust, spitting into the pool.

Mental note, Adrienne thought. *Do NOT get in the pool.*

"Okay," she said. "That works for me. Just make sure everything is set up by ten forty-five."

"You bet, Nanny," he said, laughing. "But you should know: I can be a much better friend to you here than Cameron Warner. By the way, did she ask for party favors?"

"Like balloons?" Adrienne asked.

"Oh, man!" Hector said, laughing out loud. "No, baby—not like balloons. If she didn't ask, don't worry about it. See you later." Hector left, and Adrienne went back to her room to change for the evening. *I have no idea what is going on here,* Adrienne realized, *but for once, I do know that I am totally out of my league.*

The pool was beautiful. Hector had set up and was tending a huge bar, and there was a table of chips, salsa, and lots of hors d'oeuvres. Tiki torches and citronella candles were lit everywhere, and slowly, guests started to arrive in private boats that pulled up to the docks behind the pool.

Cameron arrived, wearing a hot pink sarong and halter top. She wore a pretty necklace with ten diamonds, which glittered next to her perfect and lightly tanned skin. "Hey, Adrienne," Cam said. "How are you settling in?"

"Great," Adrienne said. "The room is nice."

"Sorry about the view," she said. "It bites. That's why I sent the clothes for you."

"They're great," Adrienne said, glancing down at the aqua and green Pucci dress she was wearing.

"That looks great on you."

"Thanks. Listen, Cam, Hector wants five hundred dollars for setting this up—"

"I know," Cameron said. "Do you mind taking care of it for now?"

"Well, I get paid tomorrow, so I guess I can lay it out for you—"

"Thanks. Don't worry, we'll settle this up when we get back to town. You won't need anything while you're here."

"Okay." Adrienne looked at all the guys and girls crowded around the pool. "This party is huge! How can we get away with it?"

"First of all, we are so far from the other house they won't even hear it. Second, they are at the Museum Dance tonight. This party will be over by the time they get home." She smiled. "Chill out. I've done this before." She peered over Adrienne's shoulder. "Oh look! There's Parker. You know him! Ciao!" Cameron scurried off.

Parker walked up to Adrienne with a big smile. "Hey,

there!" he said, and gave her a big kiss. "Adrienne! How cool that you're here! I hate these kids."

"They seem okay to me," Adrienne said. "It *is* nice to see a familiar face, though."

"Tell me about it," Parker said. "So, have you talked to Liz?"

"Not since I got here. She said she had a great time with you at Khmer."

"We did. At least, I think so, too," Parker said.

Adrienne smiled. *I can't wait to call Liz to tell her Parker likes her,* she thought.

"Hey, come on over to the pier. Bandar and Achim are here, and Mimi will be here as soon as she's done having dinner with her family at the Breakers."

"Cool," Adrienne said, following him over to watch the other kids arrive at the pier.

An hour later, Cameron stood on a chair to make an announcement. She seemed to already have had a bit too much to drink. "Hey, everyone! This is just a little party to get you all ready for tomorrow night. My parents are out, and we're going to have a big party up at the Villa!"

"Woooo!" screamed the crowd. "All right, Cameron!"

"All right?" Cameron shouted. "I'll show you all right!" She slipped off her halter, dropped her sarong, and stepped completely naked, except for her Manolo Blahnik shoes, into the swimming pool.

Everybody went wild.

Adrienne looked around. It was suddenly out of control. Bandar and the other guys were ripping off their clothes to get into the pool with Cameron. Adrienne had lost Parker. She searched the crowd for him. Suddenly, she saw him.

He was in the hot tub.

With Princess Mimi von Fallschirm.

Naked.

What the hell is going on? One minute he's telling me he likes Liz, and the next he's in the hot tub with Mimi? This is totally not cool at all, Adrienne thought. This was unlike any party she had ever been to. Everything was moving way too fast, spinning out of control. She felt lost. *I'm getting out of here,* Adrienne decided.

Sneaking away, she headed toward the Lake House and ran into Hector.

"Good party," he said. "Don't worry, I'll clean up."

"Uh, thanks," Adrienne said.

"Want to come to my room?" Hector said. "I have some pot there."

"Thanks, but no thanks. I . . . uh . . . need to be up early," she lied, scooting around him, her heart pounding.

"Suit yourself!" he called after her, laughing.

Turning the corner, Adrienne ran smack into Graydon, who was on his way down to the pool, carrying a bottle of champagne and wearing a robe. "Looking for me?" he asked with a naughty smile.

"Um, just heading back," she said, trying to escape.

"Are you sure you're not looking for me? I have a treat for you . . . ," he said, slowly opening his robe.

Without looking down—there was no way she was going to check if he had a suit on!—Adrienne summoned every last bit of cool she had left. "No, Graydon. I'm not looking for you or for any 'treat' you might have to offer me." She pulled herself up to her full height and walked into the house like a queen.

Once inside, she slammed the door behind her and put her back up against it.

Palm Beach is a nightmare! she thought as she climbed the stairs to her room. *I can't wait to tell Liz.* She suddenly came to a complete halt, mid-stair, with a horrible thought.

But how can I tell Liz about Parker and Mimi?

CHAPTER THIRTEEN

on the cover of
a magazine

Liz pushed back her bedroom shade and gazed out her rain-splattered window. She could see a sliver of the early morning gray sky between the two brick buildings across the way. The day looked to be rainy, cold, and horrible. She slipped back into bed and pulled her comforter up, over her shoulders. *Maybe I'll just stay here all day,* she thought. *It's Saturday.*

"Oh no!" Liz groaned. Today was the day of Dr. M-C's interview with *New York* magazine. Liz had to be at her apartment at noon to watch the kids. She glanced at the clock on her night table. *Three more hours of freedom,* she thought, sinking her head back onto her pillow.

She closed her eyes and thought of Parker. Yesterday at the museum had been so perfect. He was great with the kids, he knew so much about art and culture, and he was the most amazing kisser ever. Liz was really hot for him, and he was obviously into her, too. Hadn't he said as much to Dr. M-C? "Liz, who I'm dating . . ." Liz sighed, and burrowed deeper into the comforter.

She wondered where their next date would be. *Maybe we'll go someplace really romantic for dinner. . . .* She could still feel the way his lips pressed against hers—almost as if he were kissing her now. *Who knows what I'll do if we're really alone and not on a street corner or in some public place?* Liz smiled to herself. She had dated a couple of guys, but going to an all-girls school like P-B had made meeting boys hard. You really had to be a girl like Cam or Mimi to get invited to the interschool parties, where you could find guys.

The phone rang, interrupting her daydreams. She looked at the caller ID. *LEWIS, ADRIEN,* it said, with a number she knew really well. She grabbed the receiver. "Hey, Adrienne! What's up? Isn't the weather gross?"

"Not exactly," Adrienne said.

"What do you mean? It's raining outside!"

"Not where I am. In Florida, it's ninety-one degrees and sunny."

Liz bolted upright in bed. "What are you doing in Florida?"

"Well, it's a long story," Adrienne said. "Yesterday, the Warners just announced they needed me to come to Palm Beach with them—right then. It's actually like they took me hostage. Mrs. Warner called my mom and got her to agree to let me come to watch Emma. I had ten minutes to race home to pack my things. Let me tell you, the place is nothing like I expected. Last night, Cameron had a pool party, and all those people from Khmer were there. There's this totally creepy pool guy named Hector, who's, like, out of *Scarface*, and Graydon is lurking around. . . ."

"Did you see Parker?" Liz asked.

"Um, yeah, I did," Adrienne said. Liz could hear the tightness in her friend's voice. "He was at the pool party. . . ." Adrienne's voice trailed off.

"Spill it, Adrienne. I can tell something happened. What was it?" Liz cringed, her mind filling with images of Cameron and Parker naked in a huge pool together. Suddenly, all the tender images of Parker were gone. She was torn with jealousy, and her stomach was killing her. "Did he mess around with someone?"

"Well, not exactly," Adrienne said carefully. "He wasn't doing anything more than anyone else at the party—"

"Well, what was he doing?" Liz asked. "Adrienne, I want to know!"

"He was in the hot tub . . . and, uh, there were other guys and girls in it with him. I wouldn't worry about it. I mean, everyone here behaved like it was totally normal. Cameron was in the pool naked with a bunch of guys, and that was out of control—"

153

"Was Cameron in the hot tub with Parker?"

"No," Adrienne said firmly. "She was not."

"Okay." Liz was silent for a moment. Suddenly, she didn't want to know every gruesome detail. She had the sinking feeling that Parker wasn't everything she was hoping he would be.

"Liz? Are you still there? Are you okay?" Adrienne asked.

"Yeah, sure, fine, great. Listen, Adrienne, I have to go. It's Dr. M–C's *New York* magazine interview today. Call me when you're back." Liz hung up the phone, her weekend ruined.

Liz entered the Markham-Collins apartment only five minutes late.

She looked around. The kitchen was still "photo-ready," and the maid was putting away the breakfast dishes.

The house was unnervingly quiet. Liz stepped into the dining room. *It's actually pretty!* she thought with pleasure. It turned out much better than Darby DuPlane had described it.

"Hello?" Liz called out into the hall. "Anyone home? Is there anyone here?"

Heather came out in a blue pinafore and a white shirt, her hair held back with a blue velvet headband. "Mommy's not ready. She's getting dressed."

"Where's David?"

"Watching TV."

"Did you guys eat?"

Heather nodded yes.

"Okay. Where's your mom?"

"Her new bedroom."

"Okay, why don't you join David? I'll be right with you." Heather nodded and skipped off.

Liz knocked on the door. "Dr. Markham-Collins?" she called. "I'm here."

"Well, it's about time," Dr. M-C said, her voice muffled behind the door. "The reporter will be here any minute. I'm beside myself. I had to get the kids dressed. Where were you?"

"I'm on time, Dr Markham-Collins, I was just . . ."

"Oh, never mind, Elizabeth. I just would have thought you would have *known* I needed you earlier. I mean, honestly, how can I be the best mother in New York City if you're not here to help?"

I would love to know that myself, Liz thought.

"Get the children. We need a meeting in the living room."

Liz rounded up Heather and David and brought them to the cheerfully designed new room.

"Okay," Dr. M-C said as she entered the room. "First, no interrupting me and no talking. *You,*" she said, turning to Heather, "will keep your smart mouth shut. No questions, okay?"

"Okay," Heather said, her lip quivering.

"And you, no complaining about the food," she said to David, who nodded, silent.

"And Elizabeth, make sure if she asks you any questions, you throw the questions back to me. I don't want the interview to be about the nanny, after all."

Dr. M-C bustled around the room. She was wearing a new outfit and glasses without the heavy, dark frames. She looked friendly, but after that performance, Liz realized that the best clothes or interior designer would never successfully disguise her true personality.

The buzzer rang, and soon they could hear the elevator door opening slowly.

"Ah, welcome, welcome!" Dr. M-C said to the two young women who entered the huge hall. The shorter of the two women dragged in a heavy wheeled case and a large tripod light. "I am Doctor Mayra Markham-Collins! Please come in and meet my beautiful children, Heather and David." She gestured for the women to enter. "Now, Elizabeth will take your coats. . . ."

Heather and David clung tightly to Liz, sensing that they were about to be left alone with their mother.

"And can we get you something to drink?" Liz asked as she draped their heavy, wet overcoats over her arm.

"Water will be fine," the taller woman said, taking a tape recorder out of her bag. "I'm Ruth Badis. I'm going to be writing the article."

"And I'm Cheryl Martino, photographer," said the other woman. She held up a camera.

"How nice to meet you. Come in! Kids, let Elizabeth take the coats away, and get some water, and we can sit down in the living room and talk."

Liz hurried into the kitchen, threw the coats on the counter, and grabbed some glasses and a bottle of Italian water. There was no way she was going to leave the kids alone with Dr. M-C. The interview would be a disaster.

"Tell me, Dr. Markham-Collins," Ruth Badis was saying, turning on her machine. "Our readers would love to know how a busy woman like you entertains her children. Where do you take them for fun?"

"For fun?" Dr. M-C asked, noticeably perplexed by the question.

Ruth turned to Heather and David and bent down so she was nose to nose with them. "Where does your mommy take you?" Heather and David stared blankly at her, as if she were speaking another language.

Liz watched the awkward silence grow longer and longer.

"David," Liz prompted, "tell them about what happens every day when your mom *picks you up from school*."

She looked at the little boy closely and nodded vigorously. He grinned. He understood she wanted him to talk about what *they* did together. "Tell them about the hamburgers," Liz said.

"After school every day," David said, "my mother takes me for a hamburger."

"Every day?" Dr. Markham-Collins said. "Oh, yes. Every day!" Dr. M-C suddenly caught on. "It's *so* important to carve out private time with each child to establish an individual relationship with them."

"What else do you do together?" Ruth asked Heather.

"She takes me to Loehmann's when we look for party dresses," Heather said. "She taught me to look for discounts and to be a smart shopper."

"But we get your clothes at Ralph Lauren—" Dr. M-C said, and then stopped herself. "For school, but it is *so* important to help children establish their individuality by letting them choose and buy their own clothes. Just because I'm well-off doesn't mean that everyone these children meet will be. It is so important to raise them outside of a bubble of privilege. Don't you think so?"

"Sure," Ruth said. She began to scribble furiously in her notebook.

Liz winced. This was going to end badly, she could tell.

"What else does she do?" Ruth asked the children.

"We go to the museum!" Heather said cheerfully.

I hope she doesn't mention Parker, Liz thought.

"We saw the Pimpled Fender!" David said. Ruth stopped writing and stared.

"The what?" Dr. M–C asked, looking directly at Liz.

"The Metropolitan Museum," Liz said. "He means the Temple of Dendur."

"That is so cute!" Ruth said, taking a sip of her water.

Ruth directed the next several questions at Dr. M–C, and Dr. M–C gave Ruth a litany of her child-rearing ideas. Liz was surprised. *A lot of them are great ideas. Too bad she doesn't do any of them with her own kids.*

Finally, the photographer began snapping pictures of the happy Markham-Collins family. Ten minutes into the photo session, she looked up from behind her camera. "I have an idea! What about one of all of you together— Mom, kids, and the nanny!"

"Of course, of course! Elizabeth, you come over here and *stand by me,"* Dr. M–C said through gritted teeth.

Oh dear, Liz thought. *I'm in trouble.* She moved over to stand next to Dr. M–C. She could feel the doctor's arm tensing slightly. The flash went off, and just as it did, Dr. M–C pushed Liz away, causing her to stumble.

"Oh, Elizabeth!" Dr. M–C cried. "Are you okay? I'm so clumsy."

"I can take another," the photographer said.

"We're fine," Dr. M–C said flatly.

The interview was over.

So much for my picture in New York *magazine,* Liz thought.

Afterward, the Markham-Collins family went to the park with the reporter and the photographer, and Liz was left cleaning up the water and glasses from the living room.

I did it, she thought as she wiped the counters. *I did a really good job. I handled the whole thing. I made this crazy family look normal!*

CHAPTER FOURTEEN

queen of france

Adrienne squinted into the blazing sunshine on the Warner's private beach. She and Cameron lay side-by-side, stretched out like cats in the sun, carefully covered with heavy sunblock. Adrienne wore a white tankini, while Cameron wore the briefest of scarlet bikinis.

Just behind them, to the left, an enormous cabana contained a bar and a buffet, tended by servants from the house. Hector was there, staring at her. She could feel his beady eyes traveling every inch of her body. How gross!

Graydon lay on a chaise nearby, snoring. Mrs. Warner didn't like to lie out, and she was having lunch at the exclusive Everglades Club with Princess von Fallschirm. Mr. Warner was tucked away in his home office. Emma sat next to Adrienne, underneath a UV-protectant tent, wearing a hat, sunglasses, and a towel over her shoulders. For light beach reading, she had a copy of *Theories of Social Behavior*.

Adrienne looked out at the turquoise water. She could get used to it here.

From her bag, her phone rang. Maybe Brian? "Hello?" she said cheerfully.

"Adrienne! Have you decided what you are going to wear tonight? My party is going to be tight! Choice crowd, *serious* music!"

Oh no, thought Adrienne, putting her hand to her suddenly perspiring forehead. *I totally forgot about her party!* "Oh, hey!" she said, as calmly as she could. "Listen, Tamara—"

"No way. You are *not* telling me that you're canceling on me," she said, a hint of anger creeping into her usually warm and friendly voice.

"I'm not canceling," Adrienne said, "but I have a really good excuse."

"And I would *love* to hear it," Tamara said tonelessly.

"Well, I had to go down to Florida. It was an emergency," she said.

"You serious?" Tamara said. "What's the matter? Your Grandma sick or something? Are you okay?"

"The Warners had to open their house this weekend in Palm Beach, and they needed me there," Adrienne explained.

"So you're telling me that you're in Florida on the beach and not coming to my birthday," Tamara said.

"It's not like that—" Adrienne began.

"It's just like that, Adrienne. That's just what it's like, you know? All right. I get it. You have fun. Just hang out with your new friends. If you keep treating me like this, they're going to be the *only* friends you've got. Later." She hung up.

Adrienne debated calling Tamara back. Just then, a servant came over and handed her, Emma, and Cameron ice-cold bottles of Evian.

"Something wrong, Adrienne?" Cameron asked, concerned.

"No. I'm okay. Thanks." Adrienne sighed, closed her phone, turned it off, and tossed it back into her bag. She would deal with Tamara when she got back to school. She didn't want to call with Cameron listening.

I'll make everything right with Tamara, she told herself. Adrienne shut her eyes and soaked in the rays. Lying there, she could hear Cameron dialing her own phone.

"Hey there, baby. How are you?" Cameron said into the phone softly. "I know! I don't feel so hot, either. It was crazy, huh? You sure had those girls going! Seriously, I thought that Chloe was going to have an orgasm right there in the pool. You're twisted." She giggled. "Excellent. I'll supply the food and the booze, you bring the rest. You're trouble, you know that? Bye, baby. See you tonight." She hung up the phone.

Adrienne rolled over. "Was that Bandar?" she asked.

"No," Cameron said, putting on her sunglasses. "It was Parker."

Adrienne didn't know what to say. What was Cameron up to? What was Parker up to?

I'd better keep my eyes on Parker tonight, Adrienne thought. *And I'd better think of a way to make this up to Tamara when I get back home.*

Emma and Adrienne watched the last half hour of a History Channel special on the Vikings.

"Don't you want to go out, Emma?"

"No," Emma said, riveted to the Viking burial process. A flaming arrow arched in the air and lit a Viking ship with a dead body on it.

"It's beautiful outside," Adrienne said, opening the shades.

"It's hot," Emma replied. "Stop bothering me. I'm watching this."

Adrienne picked up her cell. She dialed Brian.

The battery symbol disappeared, and the phone shut down. *Always when you need it,* Adrienne thought, *the dumb thing dies.* "Do you mind if I make a phone call from here?" Adrienne asked Emma.

"No," Emma said. "Anything to get you to shut up."

Adrienne stuck out her tongue at Emma, who rolled her eyes. Adrienne picked up the phone and dialed Brian's cell.

"Cameron?" he said excitedly.

Stunned for a minute, Adrienne paused.

"Hello?" Brian said.

"It's me," Adrienne said flatly.

"Hey! Adrienne! Even better!" he said. "I saw the caller ID. It said, '*Warner Palm Beach*.' I assumed—"

"That *Cameron* was calling you? Fine. Just fine," Adrienne said, unable to mask the shock and hurt in her voice. "Well, I guess you've figured out I'm in Palm Beach."

"That's so cool! Is Cameron showing you a good time?" he asked.

He's been talking to Cameron! Cameron has been calling him! Adrienne thought. *I can't believe this!*

"Hello? Adrienne? Are you there?"

"I'm here," Adrienne said flatly.

"Is the house huge?" Brian asked. "Cameron told me about it."

"When?" Adrienne demanded.

"Um . . . at the recording studio."

"You're lying," she said. "I can always tell when you lie." Adrienne could feel her chest tightening. Suddenly, there wasn't enough air in the room.

"Adrienne, okay, she called this morning to say you guys were having a good time and that she was taking care of you. Hey, I'm the one who should be jealous—she told me all about the wild party you threw last night."

The party I threw? Adrienne thought. *He's really got to be kidding!*

"You know what?" Adrienne said. "It looks like Emma is about to fall into the pool. I have to go." She hung up on him. She was shaking.

"Hey, I'm right here," Emma said. "You didn't need to hang up."

"She totally needed to hang up," Cameron said, walking into the room. "You shouldn't tie yourself down with one guy, Adrienne. You've never looked better, and you've certainly never had access to the guys you'll meet at the party tonight. Listen, Adrienne, my brother is hot for you, and believe it or not, he's really great. Also Jaime—he's the heir to a Venezuelan oil fortune—and Jean-Charles, who is third in line to the French throne—"

"France doesn't have a throne," Adrienne muttered.

"It might again one day—you never know with France. You'd make a really nice queen," Cameron teased. "Listen, it's the opening party of the season here tonight. Let's get you dressed up." Cameron headed toward the French doors.

"Cameron!" Adrienne said sharply. Cameron whirled around. Adrienne was so angry, she wasn't sure if she would make any sense. But she didn't really care. "We *have* to talk—"

"Not now, Adrienne. I have to get ready for the party

tonight. I hope you'll be there." With a little wave, Cameron waltzed out the door.

Oh, I'll be there, Adrienne thought. *I'm not letting you out of my sight.*

CHAPTER FIFTEEN

trust me . . .

The party at the Big House was incredible. The night was so beautiful. Chinese lanterns filled with candles hung on all the trees, and the tables were covered with beautiful bouquets of flowers. This wasn't like a party that kids threw when their parents weren't home—this was like a wedding.

Everyone was either talking or dancing, but Adrienne just stood in a corner, staring into space. A bunch of cute guys came over to meet her, but none of them were as cute as Brian, she thought. Adrienne was torn—she couldn't stop being incredibly angry at him, but she couldn't stop missing him either.

"Isn't this the best?" Cameron said, walking up to her. She looked gorgeous in her patterned pink-and-aqua Versace dress.

"Totally amazing, Cam," Mimi gushed by her side.

"It's great," Adrienne muttered. She was still furious, but she didn't want to get into it in front of Mimi.

"What is *wrong* with you?" Cameron whined. "You're bringing me down, Adrienne. What's the problem? The night is great, the place is running hot and cold million-aires, and you look amazing!"

Adrienne sighed. She did look good. Cameron's pink organza Dior was gorgeous on her. "I'm just not in the mood."

"Come with Doctors Warner and Fallschirm, Miss Lewis." Cameron and Mimi pulled Adrienne into the house and up the stairs to Mrs. Warner's bathroom.

Adrienne stepped into the bathroom and her mouth dropped open. The huge pink marble room had a Jacuzzi, a steam bath, a sauna, a shower, and a whole dressing area. Cameron opened a mirrored door to reveal an entire phar-macy of pills.

"Does something hurt, or are you just tense?" Cameron asked in a professional tone.

Adrienne's stomach tied up in knots. She was not about to do Mrs. Warner's drugs. "Just tense, Cam. Come on, let's go." Adrienne moved toward the door.

"Here you are," Cameron said, taking a pill from one of the bottles and handing it to Adrienne.

"What is it?" she asked.

"Trust me, you'll be fine. My mother lives on these, and so do I. I'd be a wreck without them. Just take it Adrienne, or go back to your room. You're the only person at this party who isn't having fun. Do you want to ruin my reputation for having the best parties in Palm Beach?"

"*Really*, it's not a big deal . . . ," Mimi said, while inspecting her makeup in the mirror. "Take it."

Adrienne looked at the tiny white pill. How bad could it be? Maybe it would stop her from feeling so lousy.

She placed it on her tongue and swallowed it. It stuck in her throat a little before Cameron handed her a glass of Evian to wash it down.

"Finally," Cameron said. "Now let's get you a glass of champagne."

The girls went back outside.

Adrienne grabbed a drink and followed Mimi to a group of gorgeous guys and girls she didn't know. Listening to them talk, Adrienne started to feel a little better.

Adrienne talked to Jean-Charles, third—or was it fourth?—in line to the French throne, and decided that he was really nice. It was worth all those years of French lessons. Jaime the Venezuelan was nice, too, and Adrienne started to smile. *I should really learn Spanish,* she thought.

A calm, warm feeling spread throughout her body. The breeze blew gently against her face, and she looked up at the stars.

I don't feel so bad, she thought. *Actually, this is terrific! The music is great! It's a lot better than Tamara's crummy party in Brooklyn!* Adrienne giggled at the thought of all her friends freezing in line outside some Brooklyn club.

"Are you all right, Adrienne?" Mimi asked. It sounded as if she were talking to her from very far away.

"I'm feeling fine, Your Highness. Fine, fine!" Adrienne said. Her head was starting to feel pleasantly light.

Within half an hour, the edge was off. After an hour, and glass after glass of champagne, Adrienne was over the edge. She was totally enjoying herself. Everyone was so cute and so interesting! Parker looked a little concerned, *but screw him!* Adrienne thought. *He's cheating on Liz! But who cares? Tonight is all about me!*

The next morning, Adrienne felt sick. But worse, she had almost no memory of the night before.

"Hey, Sleeping Beauty!" It was Cameron, walking in and sitting on the corner of the bed. "How are you feeling?"

"Ugh," Adrienne replied. "Where's the cat?"

"What cat?" Cameron asked.

"The one that crapped in my mouth when I was asleep," Adrienne said, and she and Cameron burst out laughing. Then Adrienne winced. She felt as if a truck had hit her.

"It was fun, wasn't it?" Adrienne asked. She hoped Cam wouldn't find out that she was so fuzzy on the details.

"You, my dear, were the star of Palm Beach. Everyone wanted to know who you were and where you came from.

I told them you were a distant cousin from Texas. Don't worry, no one knows you're the nanny."

"Thanks, Cameron," Adrienne said, falling back into bed. "Oh." She sat back up. "You said you'd pay me back the five hundred . . . and I really need it."

"Of course," Cameron said. "Remind me again when we get home. But then again, you might not still be the nanny when we get back. You were supposed to be with Emma half an hour ago. My stepmother is not happy."

Adrienne looked at the clock. *Shit!* She raced to get dressed and get to Emma's room.

"Hey!" Emma said, smiling cheerfully, when Adrienne opened her door. Emma sat at the computer. CNN was on. Everything was normal.

"Want to see the pictures I took?" Emma asked.

"Sure," Adrienne said, thrilled that whatever Emma was doing didn't involve noise or a Viking funeral. *Though,* she thought, *a Viking funeral might be preferable to the way I feel.* Adrienne crossed over to the computer and sat down.

"Ready?" Emma said. "I'm going to start the slideshow."

The pictures appeared one by one:

Adrienne dancing.

Adrienne and Cameron at the karaoke machine.

Adrienne smiled. *I look good,* she thought. *I remember all of this.*

Cameron making out with a guy from some WB

show. Adrienne giggled. *Cam is so busted!*

Adrienne dancing on a table. *Oops. I don't remember that at all,* Adrienne thought.

Adrienne in the pool in Cameron's dress. Adrienne gasped. Where was the dress now? She couldn't remember.

Adrienne being dried off by . . . Graydon!

Adrienne making out with Graydon.

Adrienne making out with Graydon—and Cameron standing nearby, laughing at her!

"Stop it, Emma! Turn it off!" Adrienne cried, her eyes filling up with tears. "How could this have happened? I don't remember any of this at all!"

"But there's *so* much more. . . ." Emma said mischievously.

Adrienne raced for the bathroom. "I think I'm going to be sick!"

CHAPTER SIXTEEN

blackmail

Adrienne walked up to Van Rensselaer High on Monday morning committed to changing everything in her life.

I made out with gross Graydon, I bailed on Tamara, and I feel like crap. She took a deep breath, crossed the threshold of the school, and headed to her locker.

Someone tapped her on the shoulder. She turned around.

It was Brian. "Hey!" he said, looking a bit bashful. "I'm glad you're back."

"I'm glad to be back," Adrienne said, pulling him to a quiet corner. "Brian, *why* were you talking to Cameron in Florida?"

Brian blinked.

"I *trusted* you." Tears started to well up in Adrienne's eyes.

"I didn't mean to hurt you," Brian said. "Nothing happened. Cam was just being nice. We're just friends."

"Brian, Cameron wasn't just being nice." Adrienne took a deep breath. She had practiced this speech a hundred times on the plane ride back from Palm Beach. "Cameron isn't a nice person. If you want to be with me, you'd better back away from her."

"Fine," Brian said. "Are we still okay?"

"I think we will be."

Brian leaned over and kissed her gently.

"Listen, I have to go. Tamara is going to kill me. I really need to make things all right with her." Adrienne hurried down the hall to Tamara's locker. Lily was there, too, talking to Tamara. Adrienne rushed over. "Tamara, I'm really sorry. The Warners wanted me down there, and I didn't have the guts to say no. So many things got screwed up. I can't have you mad at me—"

Tamara interrupted. "Honey, don't worry. There is only one thing I want."

"What's that?"

"I just want my friend back. I don't know you anymore."

Adrienne nodded. Tamara was right.

Adrienne didn't know herself anymore, either.

That afternoon, Adrienne entered the Warners' apartment feeling more confident than she had that morning, but still a little nervous. The apartment was quiet, except for Bisquit, who came out to greet her. "You are the only normal thing in this house," she whispered to the dog. He barked and ran away.

"Hey, gorgeous you! Come on in, my favorite partner in crime!" Cameron walked across the hall to meet her. "People can't stop talking about the party, and they can't stop talking about you! It was so much fun. I decided— now stop me if you think I'm a genius—that we are going to transform you into an heiress. I'll teach you everything you need to know to get along in society. I'll teach you how to walk, how to sit, who went to what school, how much money everyone has . . ." Cameron continued, detailing the heights to which Adrienne would climb under her tutelage.

Adrienne interrupted her. "Cam," she said with her newfound sense of self, "I already know how to walk and how to sit. We had a great time, but I'm your sister's nanny. I think we should draw the line. I'll never fit in with your crowd, and I want you to back off from my boyfriend. Okay?"

Cameron stared at her. "What?" she said calmly.

"I said back off Brian, Cam."

Cameron stepped back and took a long, careful look at Adrienne. "That's Miss Warner to you, Nanny Lewis. I wanted to be nice to you and your idiot boyfriend, but if you want to still work here, you'd better watch your ass.

I don't think the Warner household needs someone who takes us for granted and uses us—"

"Uses *you*?" Adrienne laughed. "Don't you think it's the other way around?"

"No," Cameron said smoothly. "The first day in this house you stole a sweater out of my closet. Then I caught you sneaking your trashy boyfriend up into *this* apartment and throwing a PARTY, which my brother and I stopped, thank God, before our parents found out. And what about the clothes you took from Bergdorf's? They were charged to my mother's account. Guess what? They weren't free. I lied. The clothes aren't in *my* closet, are they? And, of course, what about paying that drug dealer, Hector, to throw a party in the servants' quarters down in Palm Beach?"

Adrienne's eyes widened. Cameron had been setting her up all along. Cameron could make it look like all those things were true.

"I never . . . I didn't . . . ," Adrienne mumbled. Until now, she had never realized just how incredibly two-faced Cameron really was. It hurt to be so betrayed.

"And," Cameron said, coming in for the kill, "what would your precious *Brian* say if he saw the photos that Emma took of you kissing my brother?"

"Hello, Adriana." Mrs. Warner entered the room. "Good to see you."

"Hi, Mrs. Warner," Adrienne said, avoiding Cameron's

icy gaze. "Thank you for the trip to Florida. It was a lot of fun. But I was just wondering when the new nanny is arriving."

"Cameron! Didn't you tell her the news?"

"I was just about to," Cameron said, her eyes glinting. "But we were too busy gossiping about Florida. Guess what, Adrienne! The nanny didn't come from London again, and we want to hire you for two more months!"

Adrienne blinked. *There is no nanny coming,* she thought. *Not now. Not ever. They just keep saying that because they know no one wants to be here any longer than they have to be.*

Adrienne looked at Cameron. Without Mrs. Warner seeing, Cameron mouthed the words, "I'm going to tell." *I can handle this,* Adrienne thought. *All I really need to do is stay clear of Cameron.*

"Okay, Mrs. Warner," Adrienne said, averting Cameron's gaze. "I can stay. That would be great."

Mrs. Warner smiled. "Wonderful. Mr. Warner and I have an important benefit Saturday night, so I'll need you to help Tania take care of Emma all day and night on Saturday. Oh, and Cameron is staying in the city this weekend, too, but she has plans, so she won't be around the apartment much. Right, darling?"

"Right!" Cameron said.

Adrienne pasted on a smile. "Sounds great."

Kane suddenly appeared, and so did the elevator. Mrs.

Warner said good-bye, stepped into the waiting elevator, and was whisked out of sight.

"So, Adrienne. Isn't it great that the new nanny couldn't make it and you get to stay on?" Cameron smirked.

"Yeah, Cam, a real laugh riot," Adrienne said.

"Oh, and Adrienne," Cameron said, looking her in the eye. "I hope you'll bring Brian around. You *know* how much I like him." She winked and left.

What a bitch, Adrienne thought.

Adrienne stepped into the kitchen with all the enthusiasm of a condemned prisoner sitting down in the electric chair.

"Hello, you!" Tania said, completely unaware of Adrienne's situation. "Miss Emma, she wait."

"Thanks," Adrienne called as she headed to Emma's room.

Emma sat at her desk, CNN was on, and Mozart played on the CD system.

"Hey, Em. How are you?"

"How are you?" Emma asked, her nose buried in a book.

"I'm not great, Emma, not so great," she replied, sitting on the bed.

"What's the matter?" Emma asked, turning away from her work.

"Do you like me?" Adrienne asked.

"Sure," Emma said.

"Then why did you take those pictures of me?" she asked.

Emma shrugged. "I don't know. I thought it would be funny. *Cam* thought it was funny."

"I didn't think they were funny," Adrienne said. "They upset me."

Emma turned back to her computer. After a few minutes, she handed Adrienne an envelope. Inside was the photo CD-ROM.

Well, at least, I have one friend in this house, Adrienne thought. She slipped the CD in her bag and let out a sigh of relief. She would make sure no one would ever see these photos! "Thanks, Emma," she said.

"No problem." Emma turned and gave Adrienne a mischievous grin. "And if you ever lose that CD, don't worry. I can always make you another copy!"

CHAPTER SEVENTEEN

"to us!"

Saturday afternoon, when Adrienne and Emma returned to the apartment from the new exhibit at the Guggenheim Museum, Adrienne found a note on the front hall table.

Adrienne,
I'm having a BIG party tonight. Need you to set up some things. Instructions are in the kitchen. Party will be a blast—invite your friend Liz. (Parker will be there.) Make sure Emma is asleep before party. Home at 8. See you then.

Ciao! Cameron

P.S. You keep my secrets, and I'll keep yours!

Adrienne tore the note in half. Somehow, her nanny job had morphed into party planning as well. But whether she liked it or not, Adrienne knew she was going to have to do what Cameron asked—until she could think of a better way out.

Adrienne asked Liz to help with the party preparations. They worked all afternoon getting the apartment ready. They moved furniture, arranged platters of food, and accepted alcohol deliveries. Luckily, Liz didn't have to watch Heather and David that day, and Emma was in her room much of the time—first with her French tutor, then with her calculus tutor.

Finally, after giving Emma dinner and a bath and saying good-bye to Tania and Kane, who were both off for the night, Adrienne tucked Emma into bed. The apartment was quiet. Adrienne gazed around. Everything was in place for the party, except the hostess herself. Adrienne had no idea where Cameron was. But she had no doubt Cam would show up soon.

Adrienne looked at herself in the front hall mirror. "I'm a wreck!" she said to Liz.

"Me, too." Liz moaned. "What should we do? Everyone will be here soon. I can't have Parker see me like this. The last time I saw him I was covered in cupcakes. I need to look good tonight—*sexy*."

Parker had been e-mailing her since he returned from Florida. Liz hadn't said anything about the hot tub, and neither had he. In fact, she had almost forgotten about it.

Well, not really, but what was important was that he said he couldn't wait to see her again, and he sounded like he meant it.

"Follow me," Adrienne said, grabbing the brightly colored duffel bags that she and Liz had brought with them. "We'll go into Mrs. Warner's room. We'll get ready there."

Once inside the bedroom, Adrienne pulled out of her bag the Dolce & Gabbana cocktail dress she had gotten during her shopping spree with Cameron at Bergdorf's. She had debated if she should wear it now that she knew that it wasn't free after all. But, in the end, she decided to go for it—next to it, everything else in her closet looked tacky.

"Oh, no!" Liz groaned, staring at Adrienne's designer dress. "I can't wear the dress I brought with me if you're wearing *that*!"

Adrienne had an idea—an idea that, a few weeks ago, she never would have considered. But a lot had changed since then.

She opened Mrs. Warner's closet door. "Let's go shopping!"

Half an hour later, Liz and Adrienne sat waiting for Cameron and her guests in the living room of the Warners' apartment. They had raided Mrs. Warners' closet and dressed Liz in Chanel and used her expensive perfume. Adrienne poured glasses of the champagne for each of them.

"To us!" Liz said. *And getting Parker!* she thought.

"To us!" Adrienne replied. *And keeping Brian away from Cameron,* she thought. Adrienne had "neglected" to tell Brian about the party tonight. He thought she was working late. There was no way Adrienne was going to bring Brian together with Cameron. Ever.

Within a few minutes, Cameron arrived, looking gorgeous. She walked around the apartment, surveying the setup. "You guys did a great job," she said appreciatively. "Honestly, my mom has hired caterers for thousands of dollars to do what you two have done practically for free!" She smiled. "You guys are the best!"

The elevator opened, and the first of an unending stream of New York's most glamorous and popular kids arrived.

An hour later Parker found Liz. "Hey!" he said, and took her by the hand. "I'm back! Miss me?"

Parker moved closer to her and kissed her deeply. Liz closed her eyes and kissed him back.

"Hey," she said, finally pulling away.

"Hey," Parker repeated, his eyes glazed and unfocused.

He's stoned again, Liz thought. She wondered if she should say something, but Parker leaned forward and began kissing her neck. His fingers moved through her hair. Liz kept her eyes open this time, staring at his gorgeous face as his lips found hers.

A few minutes later, it was Parker who pulled away. "Listen, I need to go talk to someone. Don't leave, okay? I really want to spend time with you."

"Who do you have to talk to?" Liz asked.

"Just a guy from school. It will only take a few minutes. Promise you'll be here?"

"I promise." She watched Parker walk toward the kitchen. He was *so* cute.

Adrienne came up to her. "Isn't this wild?" Adrienne shouted over the noise. The music was loud, the champagne and cocktails flowing. Mimi was dancing on a table with Bandar, and there was a huge line for the bathrooms.

"Exactly what I expected!" Liz shouted back. "These kids are animals."

Liz looked around the room at all the beautiful teens in their designer clothes. The hip-hop music pulsed, and Liz rocked to the beat. She gazed at the crowd around the bar and sucked in her breath. She thought she saw . . . *no, it can't be him,* she told herself.

She took a few steps to her left, to get a better view, but he had disappeared. Or maybe he was never here. Liz had to find out.

"I'm going to look for Parker," Liz told Adrienne. Liz forced her way through the crowded living room and library and hall, all the while searching not for Parker, but for *Brian. What is Brian doing here? Adrienne didn't invite him!*

185

Could Brian really be at this party without telling Adrienne? The thought of it seemed kind of ridiculous. But she was pretty sure she had seen him by the bar.

Liz searched all the party rooms and couldn't find Brian anywhere. Catching sight of herself in the front hall mirror, she realized that her lip gloss was gone. *I'll duck into Cameron's room,* she thought. *The lines for the bathrooms are way too long.*

Liz opened the door and walked into the quiet hall that led to the bedrooms. Emma was asleep in hers, so she tiptoed quietly. She carefully opened the door to Cameron's bedroom and took a step inside. Then she stepped out quickly.

Cameron was in there. On the bed. Making out.

With Brian!

"Oh, my God!" shrieked Adrienne, who had just come up behind her.

Liz shut the door. Adrienne opened her mouth to speak, but then turned and ran down the hall. Liz hurried after her friend. She found Adrienne pressed into a corner just past Emma's room.

"It'll be okay," Liz said softly to her friend.

"No, it won't," Adrienne said, taking a deep gulp of air.

"Don't worry, we'll figure out what you should do." Liz grabbed her friend's hand and led her back down the hall. "But you can't hide here. If you do, Cameron will know she upset you. You have to pretend to be strong—at least for a little while."

Adrienne nodded and wiped her tears. She took a steadying breath. Together, they headed to the living room.

"Okay, everyone!" Cameron appeared. She stood on a marble tabletop so people could see her. "There are limousines downstairs to take everyone, and I do mean EVERYONE, out to Vapor!" The kids roared. Vapor was the hottest club in town. Cameron had called cars to take everyone less than two blocks away. "You're all on the list!" Cameron called. "Let's get moving!"

Everyone streamed out of the apartment, leaving their glasses, their half-eaten food, and a big mess behind.

Adrienne, Parker, and Liz were the last to reach the elevator door, where Cameron was standing in one of her mother's floor-length sable-fur coats. "Come on, you guys, get in!" Cameron said cheerfully, pulling Parker into the elevator.

Adrienne pressed her hands on the front hall table, watching Cameron. She willed herself not to cry again. She would never cry in front of Cameron.

"Aren't you coming?" Mimi called to Adrienne and Liz from the packed elevator.

"Adrienne can't come," Cameron said. "She has to stay here and clean up this mess up."

"I am *not* cleaning up your mess!" Adrienne said.

Cameron stepped out of the elevator. "*My* mess? I don't think so. You're the one my stepmother left in charge here tonight. *I* didn't have a party. *I* wasn't even home. So I think that it is *your* mess, isn't it?" she said with a sneer.

Adrienne stood aghast as Cameron slithered deep into the crowded elevator. Hiding in the back, she could see the top of Brian's head. Adrienne wanted to scream. But all she could do was stare. At her cowering boyfriend—with Cameron.

The elevator door closed, leaving Adrienne and Liz with the wreckage of the party.

CHAPTER EIGHTEEN

"you're fired!"

*B*ack to the Present

How on earth did I get into this mess? Adrienne asked herself again as she sat on the floor of Mrs. Warner's closet. The diamonds were gone. Stolen!

Adrienne heard the elevator open in the entry hall.

"The building's private security force is here," Emma said, still standing in the closet doorway. "I think you better get up off the floor."

Adrienne stood and took a deep breath. Then she and Emma hurried from the bedroom into the front hall. Four security men, dressed all in black, and Reilly, the doorman, stood by Liz in the entryway.

"Anything wrong, Miss Lewis?" Reilly asked.

In a shaking voice, Adrienne told her story, and the security men began to search the apartment for clues.

"Don't worry, Miss Lewis," Reilly said kindly. "We'll have it all sorted out."

"Will you tell Mr. and Mrs. Warner?" she asked.

"Let's see what happens first," he said.

An angry buzz came from the elevator.

"Residents downstairs," Reilly said. He got back into the elevator and disappeared downstairs.

"I'm going to take Emma into the kitchen," Liz whispered to her. "Give her some milk or something."

"Thanks," Adrienne said, so incredibly glad that her best friend was there.

Once Liz and Emma left, Adrienne went into the living room. The lights were blazing as the security detail pored over the apartment. They opened all the curtains she had closed, to see if the windows had been tampered with. They were moving furniture and looking behind paintings, leaving them askew. Adrienne prayed she could put it all back in order.

She returned to the hall, pulled out her phone, and began to dial her home number to ask her mother for advice. As the phone rang, she stared ahead into space toward the elevator.

Adrienne watched the numbers: 9 . . . 10 . . . 11 . . .

There is no way it can be the Warners, she thought. *It's way too early.*

12 . . . 14 . . . 15 . . .

Oh, no. It is. I'm dead, she thought. She closed her phone.

PH . . . DING!

The doors of the elevator opened, and Cameron Warner stepped into the front hall.

She was drunk—no doubt about that—but still gorgeous. Her pink organza Chanel minidress was ragged and looked like it had been splashed with something. Her Jimmy Choo shoes were ruined, but her makeup, hair, and posture were, as always, perfect.

"Oh! Adrienne, *darling!*" she said, her eyes focusing. "How divine that you're home! Run and get some pink champagne from the wine cellar—it matches my outfit, right?" Cameron reached out for support, grabbing Adrienne's bare shoulder with an icy hand. "I am so wasted," she said.

She stepped out of her dress and left it on the floor, standing in the hall in her bra, stockings, and high heels.

"Oh," she said, smiling sweetly. "You can have that Chanel dress. Bandar threw up on it, but if you dry-clean it, it'll probably be fine. I can't wear it again, that's for sure—Page Six got a picture of me in it." She tottered down the hall toward her bedroom.

DING!

The elevator door suddenly opened again. Adrienne turned around. Standing there, framed in the light, were Mr. and Mrs. Warner, back early from their benefit.

Mrs. Warner slipped her mink coat from her shoulders

and silently handed the coat to her husband, who grinned stupidly. She walked across the marble floor slowly, her Manolo Blahnik heels clicking deliberately as she drew closer to where Adrienne stood. She took in the fact that the lights in the apartment were all blazing, the curtains open, and the furniture in disarray.

"Adrienne," Mrs. Warner said quietly, suddenly able to remember her name. Her eyes glittered as brightly as her emeralds. "I've had a little conversation with our security force, and it appears we have a problem. I'm not quite sure how to handle it, but I can start by saying, you're fired."

CHAPTER NINETEEN

going back . . .
and getting him back

"Honey, you've been on the sofa all day. It's almost four o'clock." Mrs. Lewis handed Adrienne a glass of Diet Coke and sat next to her.

Adrienne groaned. "Mom, leave me alone." Adrienne had spent most of Sunday curled up in bed. She had refused to answer even Liz's phone calls. She had convinced her mother to let her skip school today. She couldn't bear seeing Brian—not yet. He hadn't even called her, that pig!

I can't believe that Cam invited Brian. I can't believe they were making out! I can't believe he went with her and left me behind.

She was having a hard time making sense out of this nightmare. She pulled a sofa pillow over her head.

She heard the phone ring, and felt her mother stand to answer it.

"Oh, hello. Yes. She is."

Adrienne pulled her head out from under the pillow. Her mother held the phone out to her.

Who is it? Adrienne mouthed.

"It sounds like a little girl."

Adrienne took the phone cautiously. "Hello?"

"Where are you? You're late. My mother will kill you, and I'm very annoyed."

Adrienne smiled despite herself. It was Emma.

"Emma, I'm sorry, but I'm not coming in. Your mom fired me because of the missing diamonds."

"Not coming in?" Emma sounded confused. "But I want you back." Emma paused. "I'm really tired of this endless procession of nannies. I mean, you weren't the greatest, but you didn't stink."

"I miss you, too, Emma," Adrienne said. "But you can call me whenever you like. E-mail me your French. I'll help you anyway."

"I don't like this at all," Emma said grimly. "I'll figure this out. I'll fix it."

I really wish you could, Adrienne thought sadly, and pulled the pillow back over her head.

Two hours later, Adrienne was still on the sofa, staring at the wall, wondering how Brian had managed to fall for Cameron.

The phone rang. It rang several times. Adrienne

listened to it ring. She wasn't going to answer it. She heard her mother snatch up the receiver in the kitchen.

Suddenly her mother hurried over, her hand over the portable receiver. "It's Mrs. Warner!" she whispered.

Adrienne shook her head. "No."

Her mother thrust the phone in her hand. "Yes," her mother said.

Adrienne glared at her mother. "Hello?" Adrienne said hesitantly.

"Hello, Adrienne," Mrs. Warner chirped. "How are you doing?"

"I'm okay," Adrienne said, wondering why Mrs. Warner was calling.

"Well, Adrienne, I have your check for last week, and some extra money for watching Emma the other night."

"Uh, thanks," Adrienne said. She took a deep breath. "Mrs. Warner, what about the diamonds?"

"It all seems to have been a bit of a misunderstanding, Adrienne. Please come by in an hour to get your money. We'll talk then. Ciao!" She hung up.

Adrienne quickly calculated how much money must be in that envelope. It was a lot, and she had earned it. She should get it, even if it meant seeing Cameron again. Adrienne got up from the sofa and headed for the shower.

She was going back to 841 Fifth—for the last time.

Adrienne arrived to find Christine Warner, elegant as always in a white Givenchy suit, standing in the middle of her living room. Her perfume filled the room, and Bisquit pranced about her feet, barking at Adrienne cheerfully, happy to see her.

"Well, hello," Mrs. Warner said, carefully crossing to where Adrienne stood in the doorway and taking her hand. "*Adrienne*," she said emphatically, "I believe I owe you an apology."

Adrienne blinked. Mrs. Warner continued. "Emma really misses you, and we'd love to have you back. And we found the diamonds."

"Where were they?" Adrienne asked.

Embarrassed, Mrs. Warner reached over to the small table nearby. On it was a folded copy of the *New York Post*.

"Emma brought this to me this afternoon, right before I called you," she said. "Read Page Six."

Adrienne opened the paper.

Flashing Heiress Feels Fine! said the caption, and above it was a picture of Cameron standing on a tabletop, flashing her underpants to the photographer. Around her neck, wrists, and on her ears Mrs. Warner's diamonds glittered.

"I guess I'll need to put a lock on my jewel cases," Mrs. Warner said. She looked at Adrienne. "Will you come back?" Mrs. Warner handed her an envelope heavy with cash.

These people are a nightmare. This job is hell, Adrienne

thought. *But the money is great, Emma's not too bad, and if I stay, I have a chance of getting Brian back.* Her mood lifted slightly. *I can keep a close watch on Cameron and figure out what she's up to.*

"Sure," Adrienne said, shaking Mrs. Warner's hand, and then petting Bisquit on the head. "Can I go and tell Emma?"

"Certainly. Oh, and Adrienne, would you be a complete dear and stay just until nine? That's when Tania comes back."

It never changes, Adrienne thought. "Sure, Mrs. Warner. No problem," Adrienne said, and turned to walk down the hall to Emma's room.

"Hey," Adrienne said cheerfully, sticking her head in the doorway. "Your plan worked. I'm back!"

Emma smiled sweetly. "Don't think it's because you are much of a nanny. I'm just tired of Mother's whims. Now, remember—it is your job to take care of me, not my job to take care of you."

Adrienne swallowed. "Well, I can always quit, if you're so unhappy. . . ."

A look of panic passed across Emma's face. "No!" she said. "I mean, I have my French homework for you to check. You might as well stay."

Adrienne smiled. "Okay. I'll stay. I'll go get you a snack. Be back in ten minutes." Adrienne left. Everything was back to normal with Emma.

As she passed Cameron's room, she took a deep breath and tried to walk by quickly.

"Hey!" Cam said. She was sitting on her suede sofa, painting her toenails with topcoat.

Adrienne gave Cam what she hoped was a look of supreme disdain and said nothing.

Cameron smiled. "So, you have your little job back, I see."

"I do," Adrienne said, "and if you don't mind . . ."

"I don't mind at all," Cameron said, "because even though you have your job back, you don't have Brian. I do."

Adrienne leaned against the doorway and gave Cameron a slow smile. "Do you *really* think so, Cameron? I wouldn't be so sure."

Adrienne turned to leave, noticing, for the first time, a flicker of doubt in Cameron's ice-gray eyes.

About the Author

VICTORIA ASHTON was born in New York and attended an elite private school. She has worked and played with the rich and famous and has seen it all—the good, the bad, and the completely outrageous. Victoria divides her time among New York City, the Hamptons, and London.

Look for Victoria Ashton's next novel,
CONFESSIONS OF A TEEN NANNY: *Rich Girls*